The Diamond and the Thief

TAYLOR ROGERS

Contents

Chapter One

The familiar whining of the alarm clock echoed through Colleen Scott's New York city apartment. Colleen rolled over in bed, her brown hair a tangled mess around her face. The early sounds of the cities' morning traffic was already drifting up to her from the streets below, a noise she had finally gotten used to after her transplant seven years ago.

She swung her arm out, fumbling for the button to silence the obnoxious noise. When she was successful, she laid there staring at the ceiling until a small round furry face popped into her view. Her cat Mochi stared into her soul with piercing yellow eyes demanding that she stop laying like a sloth and get up to fill her food bowl. It was only when the gentle kneading against her chest started including sharp pokes of small razor-sharp claws did Colleen concede and swing her legs over the side of the bed and march into the bathroom. The small striped tabby padding along behind her. She showered quickly; the small bathroom always filled with steam fast so while it defogged, she filled the small pink food bowl on the floor by the counter that had the smallest bit of the bottom showing.

"Yes, I'm sure *Arms of an Angel* is playing in the background like an ASPCA commercial." Colleen said as her cat investigated the bowl to make sure it was sufficiently filled.

With the beast appeased Colleen moved back into the muggy windowless bathroom to finish getting ready for work.

One of the perks of working in the diamond district was that her boss made sure she got one hell of a discount so that way she could be a walking billboard for his store. Today she put on a high-end AAA quality Akoya pearl strand with matching studs and bracelet to complement the dark navy skirt suit she had pulled out of her small closet. Her classic black stilettos were secured in a tote bag she kept by the door next to a pair of comfy slip-on sneakers she would wear until she got to work. She always said the jewelry was worth the toe pain but she'd be damned if she walked the busy streets in those torture devices. The filth that could accumulate on the city sidewalks had already claimed enough of her expensive work shoes when she was fresh to the city and inexperienced.

With a sneak attack kiss onto Mochi's head Colleen snagged her tote bag and was out the door.

She lived on the second floor of her apartment building so she always used the stairs, it was her excuse for never setting foot in the gym they had on the corner of the block. For once, luck had been on her side, and the apartment she had was close to work. God. Forbid she'd have had to take the subway to work, or worse, a taxi. Walking was far more preferable in her opinion, questionable as the sidewalks were.

Besides, the small coffee shop on the way had one of the best blueberry bagels she had ever tasted. Carlos who worked the counter always had her breakfast and latte ready to go so that way she was in and out in the time it took her to wait in line and tap her phone to pay. In return she got him a great deal on the diamond stud he wore in his ear.

"Good morning Lina." He sang out in his thick Puerto Rican accent. The diamond glinted in the light that came in from the wall of windows. He was also the only person who called her Lina.

"Good morning. Carlos. How are you?"

"Good, good. Here you go, fresh and hot from the oven. I even threw on the new honey infused cream cheese we are trying out. You'll have to let me know what you think." Carlos pointed at the bagel in her hand before turning to help the next customer in line.

"Carlos you are an angel." She blew him a kiss and tucked a five in his tip jar. He shot her a wink and turned back to the older gentlemen who had walked in behind her.

Outside Colleen peeled back the wrapping of her bagel in one hand while balancing her iced coffee in the other. A glorious amount of cream cheese was layered between the halves and Colleen almost groaned right there on the sidewalk when she took the first bite. She was going to have to start going to that corner gym because this was definitely going to be added to her daily order. She was careful with her bites, not wanting to risk anything spilling out of the bagel and landing on her clothes.

She glanced down at her watch and smiled as she slowed her normally quick pace. It was mornings like this, when she could take a few extra minutes on her walk to work to enjoy her breakfast and take in the morning sites of the city. She glanced into some of the shops that weren't open yet for the day. Some of them had dim lights on, staff milling around organizing and stocking. The sidewalk was filling up with the morning rush crowd that also walked to work and the traffic on the road was already at a standstill. The city had an energy about it today, probably due to the good weather finally deciding to stick around. Colleen smiled, it was going to be a good day today, she could feel it.

Chapter Two

By the time she reached the store front her bagel and ice coffee were both gone and disposed of on the way. She rapped her fist against the metal security cage that pulled down from the building just below the old wooden, hand painted sign for 'Campbells Jewelry' and waited for Roger to come let her in. A chorus of locks unclicking sounded before an older gentleman with a mass of receding gray curls came out and stooped to grab the cage and lift it into the air with a groan.

"One of these days Roger you're not going to be able to lift that and will finally have to get an automated one like everyone else." Colleen teased, knowing the older man despised anything and everything automated.

"That will be the day I sell this place and retire. Those newfangled self-opening doors will let God knows who in." Roger groused back good naturally.

Colleen walked in shaking her head and chuckling at her boss, the sound of the metal rolling back to the concrete followed her. They both knew Roger wasn't even close to ready to retire, no matter how many times he threatened too.

If it wasn't for modern society forcing him to take card payments, Roger would be happy with solely taking cash still. When their credit card processor company sent the device that enabled them to take payments from cards saved on phones, Roger grumbled away in his office for two days. He still refused to learn how to use it.

Campbells was a small jewelry store, started by Roger's dad in the Fifties. Roger's son David who worked the evening shifts was set to inherit the store as soon as Roger finally decided to retire. Colleen had worked there for seven years; ever since she moved to New York after college. The store had a perimeter of glass display cases in the show room with a small circular one in the center that had a space just large enough for two employees to stand in the middle to pull items out. A small workshop could be seen through a window near the back wall where Roger would sit to size rings and set stones in pieces that were sold or designed to show off in the case. An office was across a small hall where they all shared a desk. Two large safes also sat in the back which held all the jewelry every night.

Colleen walked to the back, the store still dimly lit. Roger preferred to wait until the last minute to turn the bright show lights on. The decreased lighting created a calming effect that Colleen appreciated. She put her tote bag down on her corner of the small desk and turned to the already opened safes and slowly began pulling trays out and marching them out to their corresponding cases.

Roger joined her, helping place the black velvet lined trays on top of the glass. Each had its own perfectly curated set of pieces that were arranged in the case together. Colleen found it fun on the slow days to rearrange and freshen up the cases. Partnering new pieces together with aged stock sometimes helped move both together.

When the last pair of diamond hoops was placed into its display, they had just a few moments left before the store was set to open. Colleen went into the office and quickly swapped her comfy sneakers for her black stilettos. She also fished a pink lipstick from the bag and used a small pocket mirror to apply it.

"Do we have any appointments today?" Colleen asked Roger as he moved to the wall with the light switches.

"There's one later this morning for an anniversary gift but other than that we shall just see how the day unfolds." He slid his hand up the wall clicking all the switches at once. "Show time." Roger sang as the store lit up. He moved back to the front and once again heaved the security cage up, this time latching it into place and pulling the blinds up for the store's front windows, letting more natural light into the showroom.

"Showtime." Colleen whispered to herself and walked out to the sales floor and greeted a young couple who strolled in arm in arm.

Chapter Three

The day had sped by, the young couple of the morning was just browsing. Roger's appointment had purchased a beautiful diamond band that he sized and had Colleen gift wrap. Later she had sold a stunning emerald bracelet to some celebrity's personal assistant who was looking for something her boss could wear to the theater that weekend. All in all, a busy, successful day.

As soon as the store was packed back away and the giant cage brought back down over the store front Colleen said goodnight to Roger's son David who had come in near the end of the day to help close shop and headed back to her apartment.

If the sidewalks were busy on her way home, they were nothing compared to the congestion that evening. With the good weather also came an uptick of tourists traveling by foot as well as the daily commuters. She stopped by the Chinese restaurant that was just a few doors down from her place to pick up her usual sweet and sour chicken and Lo-Mein combo for dinner. The food was good, and the couple that owned it believed in healthy sized portions that Colleen liked for the ease of packing the next day's lunch.

When she walked in Mochi came up meowing and demanding attention, and for the empty spot in her bowl to be filled again.

After filling the bowl and giving several cuddles to the small cat before she squirmed away, Colleen dressed down into a comfy set of sweats and threw her hair into a messy bun. After settling on the couch with her order and a glass of white wine she turned on her tv and flipped through the channels for something to watch. The news was playing on one channel reporting a string of burglaries across the river in Jersey that had gone unsolved and the police were unclear if they were connected or separate. Colleen clicked through preferring to find something to remove her from the tragedies of regular life. She flashed through a few reality shows before finding an older rom-com movie and settled in for the night.

When the wine glass was empty and her left over food was put in the fridge for lunch tomorrow Colleen moved to the bedroom where she layed in bed doom scrolling on her phone. She gazed at her friends posts and photos on their engagements, babies and family vacations. Liking them to show her support, but there was the ever-present twinge at feeling like she was falling behind in her life. Yes, she had a great job, and was living the small-town dreams of her child-hood friend group of living in New York, buying expensive clothes and shoes whenever she wanted. But still, here she was- alone, watching other people's lives through her screen until she finally fell asleep.

The next morning Colleen's alarm clock buzzed against the city noise waking her from dreams of work. She laid there for a moment disgusted in her own boring dreams. *Really, your dreaming of sorting through gemstones* she thought to herself. She was just about to get up when she felt the small weight of Mochi who was contently still snuggled beside her. Apparently happy to lay there all morning like they usually did on her days off. But today was Thursday, and unfortunately not one of those days. Colleen slowly wiggled out of the bed, the grumpy feline stretched out and kneaded at the duvet with her claws out. Colleen winced at the snapping sound of the small razors snagging threads.

"Will you stop that! I have to go to work Mo's."

The cat just glared at her, her pupils dark slits. Suddenly the phone on Colleen's nightstand vibrated against the wood, the sound sending the irritated feline streaking out of the room. Picking up the silent phone Colleen saw *Mom* light up on the screen.

"Ugh it's too early for this." Colleen groaned. She loved her mother, and she knew she should have initiated a call with her days ago, but her mom had a way of sucking Colleen's soul out through the phone. She would undoubtedly try anything she could to get Colleen to move back home. But she gritted her teeth and slid her finger along the bottom of the phone to answer.

"Hey mom" Colleen greeted and moved to fill Mochi's food bowl. The cat hidden away in one of her secret spots that Colleen couldn't find. Though the feline came strutting across the living room seemingly out of nowhere as soon as she heard the clink of kibble hitting her bowl.

"Good morning honey, just checking in because we haven't heard from you in a while. How's it going?" Her mom's voice holding the slightly accusatory tone Colleen knew well and had predicted would come out.

"I'm good, just getting ready for work. How's it going? How's dad?" Colleen knew from years growing up with her parents that her mom had the phone on speaker and her dad was in fact silently sitting nearby, listening but not participating in the conversation.

"Oh everything is good and he's just fine. Busy working. So, I was just wondering…"

Here it comes Colleen thought.

"Gary's son George, you remember George?"

"Yes, I remember George." Colleen gritted out through clenched teeth. This was worse than just the normal 'you should come visit more often' speech. This was going to involve poking into Colleen's love life too.

"Well George recently broke up with his girlfriend Tiffany. Which if you ask me is a blessing in itself, she was a *terrible* woman." Her mom's childhood southern accent accentuated the word terrible. Colleen could practically see her mom's hand going to her chest in dismay.

"Mom that's not nice, she wasn't terrible." While she didn't know Tiffany personally, coming to a stranger's defense against her mom was just a knee jerk reaction.

"She flossed in public Colleen. Right there in the middle of the store. What would you call that?" Her mom said flatly.

Colleen shrugged; her mom had a point there.

Taking Colleen's silence as answer enough, she continued.

"See I told you. Anyway, George is now a free man and I was thinking maybe the two of you can hang out when you come home to visit."

"Mom, first of all I live four states away. And I'm not coming home to visit until thanksgiving, and it's April. Even if I wanted to see George, I'm sure he will have found someone else by then." Colleen rolled her eyes as she fished her outfit for the day out of the closet and laid it on the unmade bed.

"Well, you don't know that now do you. And I really wanted you to come home for the Fourth of July. You really need to visit more often..." Her mothers tone was getting to that accusatory pitch that was the sole reason why Colleen hadn't instigated any calls.

"Okay mom, we've been over this and I have to get ready for work. I love you, good bye." She was not wanting to have this conversation again.

"Good bye sweetie." Colleen could hear the frustration in her mom's voice.

"Good bye, mom."

Colleen tapped the screen to hang up the phone, already mentally drained with the day.

She moved to the bathroom and began her morning routine trying to shake the exhaustion, and the tension that always built up in her neck from speaking to her mother.

She loved her parents but there was a reason she had chosen a college out of Kentucky and moved to New York immediately after. The diploma had barely been placed in her hands when she rented the apartment, she had now sight unseen and applied for the position at Campbells. And for the most part her parents understood, they knew she made decent money here and was happy. But Colleen's singleness was the constant blight in her mother's life. Especially when her brother, who was two years younger than her was happily settled with a wife, three kids, and a golden retriever in the suburbs of her hometown.

The dating pool in New York was vast but it was like picking through gravel to find her diamond. But at almost thirty Colleen would settle for a well-made quartz at this point.

The last guy she'd been on more than two dates with had been pleasant and courteous on the dates they went on. He had been gloriously more than nice and courteous when she'd brought him back to the apartment one night. But the next morning Mochi was in a hissing, spitting fit, which wasn't uncommon for her when meeting strangers. But when Colleen caught the guy trying to kick her like a soccer ball, only missing because Mochi had the speed of a race car, she shoved him out the door with his shirt in his hand and told him not to call her again.

After that last experience Colleen had decided to take a break from dating. She now spent her nights with Mochi, and an order of take out while watching the reality shows following yacht crews. And she was content with her life, for the most part.

Her morning was behind from the phone call, so Colleen had to rush to get dressed. She packed her leftovers from dinner into her bag with a pair of red heels to pop with her black slacks and matching silk blouse. She folded her blazer into her bag but snagged her leather jacket out of the closet as she walked out the door.

Chapter Four

That morning Carlos had given her one of their plain bagels with cinnamon cream cheese. Paired with her latte it was a comforting combination of spices. After Roger let her in, she put her lunch in the small mini fridge and started pulling things out of the safe.

"We have some new sapphires that were delivered this morning. I think we should put them near the front." Roger pointed to a tray sitting on the check-out counter by the shop window that allowed customers to peer into shop and watch Roger work while they paid.

"Sounds good to me." Colleen walked over to review the new pieces. Bright royal blue pear-shaped sapphires alternated directions in a row surrounded by small brilliant accent diamonds. The set consisted of a bracelet, collar style necklace and chandelier earrings. They also came with a pretty price tag, definitely on their higher tier. They were beautiful.

Grabbing the tray Colleen took the exquisite new pieces up to the front case, admiring how they flashed and sparkled even in the dim morning light of the store. She used special risers and a long lay down neck ramp to really enhance the display of the suite. During the day customers walking by on the street would be able to glance in and see them.

Stepping back to admire her work Colleen glanced to the case next to it and was now unhappy with its configuration. It now looked drab in comparison.

Sighing, she moved on to start reworking the whole store. Roger chuckled as he brought the rest of the trays out and set them on top of the glass cases. He put their engagement ring cases away before retreating to his shop to work on a custom order they had gotten a few days ago.

After changing around the displays to allow the product to flow better for the shopper's experience Colleen moved on to wipe down the finger prints from the top glass in the final moments before the store opened.

As the she wiped the last one down the overhead lights flicked on.

"Showtime!" Roger sang as he walked by and admired the new set up on his way to raise the gate, his jeweler goggles resting on top of his head, pushing his grey hair out in odd angles.

"I'll be in the back most of the day. We took in quite a few sizing's so I'm going to see if I can knock all those out this morning so they can get picked up before the end of the week. And then try to finish that custom pendant."

"Okay sounds good." Colleen went to switch out her flats and donned the blazer from her bag.

Most of the morning slid by slowly. A few people came in to browse but only one ended up buying a small pair of silver cuff links. He had been young, in a suit almost too big. Colleen could tell he must have just gotten his first pay check from whichever business firm he was at and was looking to add a little accessory to his daily attire. Colleen always liked these kinds of customers. Today it was a small silver purchase, but tomorrow it may be a diamond engagement ring for his girlfriend.

By lunch time Colleen peeked in on Roger who was just finishing another sizing.

"Can you call them and let them know it's ready for pickup?" He asked handing her the envelope with the customers information.

"Yeah, no problem." She grabbed it from him, careful to avoid the black polishing compound that stained his fingers from the tools and made her way to the store phone.

"I'm going to run down to the bodega to grab a sandwich. Want anything?" Roger asked standing up from his work bench and stretching his back.

"No, I brought some food to heat up. But thank you."

"Alright, I'll be right back." He walked out the front door and turned to go down to the corner market. His goggles pushed up, but still on his head.

The number Colleen called clicked to voicemail so she left a message letting them know their item was ready for pick up and went to file it back in the safe. She snagged her leftovers on the way back near the front counter and popped it into the microwave keeping an eye out to the show room.

Right as the microwave beeped the chime of the front door echoed in the back. Colleen quickly hit the button to shut it up before turning and heading back up front to help the customer.

She was looking down making sure her blouse was straightened as she walked under the bright lights. She glanced up smiling to greet the person, but was startled to see no one there.

Confused Colleen walked to the center case to try to look out the front windows to see if maybe there was a kid or one of the streets many unhoused had tried to come in.

No one was on the sidewalk out front.

Colleen moved closer to the door to see if maybe the old doors sensor was stuck from when Roger had left. Just as she passed the edge of the front case a dark figure appeared from the corner of her vision. Before she could even let out a gasp a strong arm had wrapped around her torso, a cold sharp blade tip pushed gently against her throat.

"You're not going to make a sound, you hear me?" A rough male voice whispered in her ear. Colleen remained silent, unwilling to even nod for fear of that blade breaking her skin.

"We are going to go over to the cases quickly now and you're going to empty them out." The arm around her released slightly and lifted up a backpack that was already unzipped. The knife moved from her throat to poking her in the lower back, just near her spine.

With shaking hands Colleen pulled her keys from her pocket and slowly walked to the front case the man was directing her to, the one she had just set up with the sapphires.

She unlocked the case door and let it drop with a bang, her hands shaking so hard she couldn't keep hold of the solid wood.

"Easy there." The man said pushing the knife a little more into her back. He looked back to the office and shop.

"No one else is here." Colleen whispered, both praying Roger would and would not show up. In his younger years Roger had been known to go toe to toe with potential thieves. Even making the newspaper once for breaking a display mirror over one's head, knocking him out cold. But at his older age Colleen didn't want to risk him trying to take on this man who from the small bit Colleen could see was quite tall and clearly enjoyed the gym from the size of his shoulders and arms.

"Well let's get this done before they decide to come back."

So, he had known there was someone else here today but waited until Roger left. That meant he had been watching them this morning.

Colleen reached into the case and carefully pulled out the contents. She turned slightly to dump the handfuls of diamonds and sapphires into the empty backpack. She winced at the sound the stones made hitting each other in the bottom of the bag.

She glanced up at the man, he was wearing all black but not in a way that would draw attention. He had a black knit cowel neck sweater that he had pulled up to cover the lower half of his face and dark wash jeans. A black leather jacket with the collar turned up and a baseball cap shadowed the rest of his identity.

"Hey come on! Next case!" He pushed the blade a little deeper into Colleen's back forcing her to turn back and move to the next case that held their supply of diamond studs. She dumped them into the bag display ramp and all.

"Come on keep going." He hurried her to the next case.

"I'm going as fast as I can, sorry that I'm slow at knife point." Colleen said with a sarcastic bite forgetting for a second the situation.

The thief chuckled and loosened the pressure of the blade slightly.

He leaned down and spoke in her ear "There, is that better?"

Colleen didn't reply, his tone irritating her now. She opened the next case of tennis bracelets and pulled them off their display. This seemed to be the last thing he was wanting as he moved the knife away and used both hands to zip the backpack and throw it over his shoulder.

Colleen glanced out the window watching silently as people walked by the shop unaware of what was happening inside just feet away.

"Now what to do with you." The man said causing Colleen to turn and stare at him, her heart feeling like it was sinking down her chest and settling into her gut. The knife still in his gloved hand appeared to be a large pocket knife, easily concealable when not in use. He reached into the outside pocket of the backpack and pulled out a pre looped zip tie.

"Stick out your wrists." The thief ordered. Colleen obliged her hands fisted closed. He flipped the knife closed and tucked it back in his jeans. Colleen watched as he looped the zip tie over her hands and winced as he pulled it tight, the thick plastic biting into her skin.

"Sorry." He mumbled and grabbed her bound wrists in one of his hands. The apology struck Colleen as odd, since he had just threatened her with a knife at her throat and back. She wondered if he had never meant to hurt her, that maybe the threat of violence was all he was aiming for.

"Sit down." He ordered pointing to the floor with his free hand. He held her hands tight and lowered her to the floor as she sank to the carpet. She looked up and caught the man's blue eyes that became visible at that angle. She looked away quickly, afraid he would be angry that she'd seen something that may help identify him later.

"Now stay here and don't get up until you count to one hundred." His tone deepened in a menacing tone. Colleen nodded and tried not to watch as he sat up from his crouch and walked to the front door. As soon as she heard the chime though she launched to her feet only to see the dark clothed figure pulling the security cage down. Earning curious glances from those with him on the sidewalk, but in true New York fashion, no one seemed to question his actions and kept going about their day.

She caught his eyes as he looked up. She couldn't see his mouth but she was sure he was smirking at her standing there clearly not counting. He wiggled his fingers at her in a wave before he turned and joined the lunch crowd that was walking by. She watched as he pulled the neck of his sweater down so that he wouldn't stand out with a face covering. She tried to catch a better look at his face but all she caught was the side of a stubble covered jaw before he walked out of site from the store window.

Chapter Five

Colleen spent the first few minutes locked in the store trying to get out of the restraints. She had first thought about opening the door and yelling for help. But she was nervous someone else unsavory would take the opportunity of her already being tied up to rob the store again.

She had just balanced one of Roger's jeweler saws on the counter and had slipped a shoe off to use her foot to anchor it in an attempt to saw through the plastic when she heard someone rattling the cage out front. Slipping out of her second heel she ran to the front and let out a sigh of relief when she saw a stunned Roger lifting the cage, his bagged lunch sitting now forgotten on the sidewalk.

"Colleen!" He yelled over the sound of the cage rattling. "What happened!"

She rushed to him as he came through the door.

"We were robbed! He came in... and he hid... and he had a knife and ..." Colleen felt like she was choking over her words as she tried to get everything out. She lifted her bound hands towards him. His eyes widened and he grabbed her by the shoulders.

"Slow down, slow down. Deep breath." He sucked air in and out his mouth trying to get her to mimic him.

"Here, let's get you out of this." He led her to the shop and stepped over her discarded shoes grabbing a pair of big snips off his bench. He slid the blades over the binding, the steal cold against her flushed skin. She flinched as he cut the piece, the tension pulling the plastic farther into her skin before it released.

"Thank you." Colleen sighed rubbing her wrist. There was a thick dark red indent on her skin. Roger walked over to the phone and dialed the police.

Within moments a few foot patrol men walked into the store and began processing the scene. They took photographs of the empty cases, their doors still open and hanging. They looked like shells of what they once were with the lights shining down on them and no return sparkles coming out.

People gathered around the front of the store, peeking in trying to see what happened. Several of them had their phones out trying to get photos or videos. Roger eventually got irritated at their presence and pulled the blinds down, blocking their view. An officer was posted at the front door to keep anyone from coming in and disturbing the scene.

The officer with the camera came over and asked to take photos of Colleen's wrists, and to ask her what had happened.

"He hid behind that case over there." She started and pointed to where the man had ducked behind the front case after he had come in. "He then jumped behind me and had a knife. He pressed it against my throat and told me to empty the cases into a backpack he had. He then held the knife to my back while I grabbed the stuff he wanted." She gestured towards her lower back. The officer leaned to look, he raised the camera and the camera shutter clicked rapidly.

"Do you mind if we take that jacket? The knife left a hole, it's unlikely anything transferred but you never know."

"Oh, um sure go ahead." Colleen shrugged out of the blazer and handed it over to the officer who took it with a gloved hand and placed it into a large evidence bag. She noticed a small hole that had been sliced along the back seam from the knife. Colleen shuttered slightly.

Roger walked over towards them, placing a comforting hand on Colleen's shoulder.

"So, you haven't seen anyone suspicious hanging around lately?" The officer asked looking at both Colleen and Roger.

"No, I mean nothing out of the ordinary that you see on the New York sidewalk any other day." Roger answered, Colleen shook her head.

The officer wrote more notes on his notepad.

Just then the front door slammed open and Roger's son David came striding through. The tails of his tan coat flapped behind him, the officer who had been posted outside followed.

"Is everyone okay?" He asked looking around at the empty cases rather than over at Colleen and his father. The officer grabbed his arm as if he were going to escort David back outside. The young Campbell pulled away and shot the officer a look of disgust.

"It's okay." Roger announced stepping forward, leaving Colleen. "He's my son."

Colleen put up with David because she enjoyed working for Roger, but she always thought the younger man was pretentious and rather spoiled. He came and worked afternoons, or whenever he thought the store would be busy and he could pull the most commission for the least amount of work. So, it really didn't shock her that his first worry was for the merchandise.

"Yes, everyone is fine David." Roger said, the officer seemed annoyed by David, but he went back outside. "Thankfully he only took a few cases of things. I was out getting some lunch when it happened and Colleen was smart enough to listen and give the man what he wanted so he left her unharmed."

David turned towards them and glanced at Colleen holding her bruised wrists.

"Well, that's good." He then turned his attention to his father. "What all was taken?" Colleen fought the urge to roll her eyes.

"I was just finishing up giving this officer my statement." Roger said in a calm tone as if he was asking his twenty-three-year-old son to wait for him to finish a phone call rather than a police report.

David clenched his jaw, clearly not happy with being told to wait.

"So, you haven't seen anyone hanging around? Maybe walking by a few too many times? Or maybe coming in and spending a long time looking around and not buying anything?" The officer by Colleen asked Roger turning away from brooding David.

"Not that I have noticed. I mean we get lookey-loos every day that come in just to browse and not buy. But I haven't noticed anyone with the normal tells of someone casing the place. Have either of you?" Roger glanced between his two employees.

Of course, David answered first.

"No, nobody has been in here acting odd, or not wanting help. At least not when I have been here. Although, if you guys could figure out how to keep all the homeless from sleeping on our stoop that would be great." David shot at the officer, who gritted his jaw and turned his back again on the store owner's son.

"What about you?" He asked in Colleen's direction.

The men all turned towards her.

"No, I haven't noticed anyone acting odd in or around the store." Colleen's nerves were shot, she twined her fingers together to try to stop the shaking that was beginning.

"And you didn't get a good look at him?" The officer scribbled more into his notebook.

"Um no, he wore a sweater with one of those big necks and pulled it up to cover his face and he kept his hat angled down to cover the rest. He was tall though, and muscular, I could tell when he moved. But there was nothing that stood out or would mark him as any different than anyone else on the street. Oh, he had blue eyes though, I caught a glimpse of them when he was putting the ties on my wrists."

"Whose height would you put him closer to?" The officer asked pointing his pen around at the men standing around her.

Colleen stood from her chair so she could compare them to her memory of when she turned to look at the thief.

Roger was on the shorter side for men, and David wasn't much taller. The officer questioning her was taller than the Campbells, with a large belly. But he too seemed to be shorter than the thief.

"I'd say he was closer to your partner's height." Colleen gestured towards the officer who was standing out front.

"Okay, and build wise, would you say his muscular structure was closer to your coworkers?" He pointed over at David who took great pride in his physical appearance and spent at least two hours a day in his special membership gym every day.

"No, I'd say he was quite a bit more muscular than David." Colleen hid the satisfaction she got from David visibly bristling at her comment. She could see Roger's mask of worry crack slightly as well at the slight.

"Well, I can tell you this robbery does sound similar to the other ones that have happened around the city. Single man targeting higher end establishments, used a knife and is in and out in under five minutes. We do believe based on there always be only one employee in when he strikes that he watches the store for a while to get his timing right."

Colleen shuttered slightly at the thought that this man could have been outside watching them for weeks and they had no idea.

"The good news is no one has been seriously hurt and he doesn't seem to strike the same place twice. We will get you a copy of the report to turn in to your insurance and we recommend maybe having more than two employees at a time if you can afford to. Just to prevent anyone from being alone in the store alone again." The officer closed his notebook and tucked it into his back pocket.

He walked over to his partner and prepared to leave.

"Thank you, officers. I really appreciate your help. Yes, I think I became too complacent with security. We haven't had an incident in the years since I took over the store so I am afraid I became too comfortable." Roger reached his hand out and shook both the officers' hands before they nodded at Colleen and David and walked out the store.

"Well." Roger said turning to Colleen. "I think you should go home and rest for a few days. I can't imagine what you must be going through. David can help me put everything away and close up the store. I need to get home and call the insurance company, let them know what happened. I'm sure they are going to want the same inventory list the officers asked me to write up." Roger's face had fallen from his normal cheery expression. Colleen gripped her twined fingers even tighter, trying to hide their increasing shake.

Colleen normally was the kind of employee that would only go home sick when forced, and even then, she made sure everything was all set before she left. But after the events of the day, she was not apt to argue. Her wrists were starting to really ache and all she wanted was to curl up in her bed and pretend the last few hours hadn't happened. She was glad she had brought her leather jacket this morning. The sun was out, but with all the buildings her walk would be mostly shaded and without her blazer now it would have been a chilly walk home.

"Okay." She replied and went to go grab her bag from the back room. She swung into the shop on the way and picked up her discarded heels.

"It's going to cost a fortune to replace the things that were stolen." Colleen heard David's voice echo back from the show room.

"Well, that is why we have insurance David. And we've never made a claim so it shouldn't affect our rates too much."

"But they will still go up. And we can't afford another employee, you'll just have to stay here and stop wandering the block for lunch." Colleen had her bag in her hand but stood shocked at how bold David was speaking to his father.

"First of all, you refuse to learn how to read the books so how would you know what we can and cannot afford. And yes, I should not have left Colleen alone, and that will haunt my nightmares tonight. I am just glad she's okay. But unless you are now offering to work full time, I will have to hire another person. And yes, that means splitting sales with another person." Roger's voice was angry and he was almost yelling.

When Colleen walked out clutching her things, she could see the father and son stood rigid and only a few feet apart.

"I'm going to head on home now." Colleen interjected; the air was thick with tension. Roger's shoulders relaxed slightly when he heard her voice.

"Do you need someone to walk you?" He turned and looked at her.

"No, I should be okay. I don't live far."

"Okay, well if you need anything please call. I will probably keep the store closed until Monday. No point in being open when half the cases are empty. So take until then. Paid, of course. And if you need any more time just give me a call and we will work something out." He gave her a small smile and fully ignored his son's anger that flashed across his face at the paid time off.

"I appreciate it, thank you so much. I hope the insurance covers everything that the man took."

"Thank you, but don't worry about this place, it will be fine."

Roger then walked her to the door and stood watch until she rounded a corner out of his sight.

Chapter Six

Colleen had walked her same route to and from the store for years and had never worried about being followed or harassed before. But that walk back from the store after the incident had the hairs on the back of her neck prickling and her constantly looking over her shoulder for anyone following her.

One particular man in a New York Rangers baseball cap Colleen noticed had followed her for a whole block. He copied her turn off the main tourist road towards her less common apartment riddled street and sent her Spidey senses flaring in alert. She quickly ducked into a small shop her heart thundering in her chest as she watched him from the shop window. He didn't even glance her way as he passed by.

Colleen had to take a few deep breaths before she was able to step back out to the sidewalk and quickly finish her route home.

A small sense of relief washed threw her when she entered her apartment building. Never before had she been so happy to see the shabby off-white walls and the rows of lockboxes for their mail. She took the stairs two at a time, her steps thundering in the stairwell.

As soon as her apartment door shut behind her Colleen flipped the lock and did what she rarely ever had done and threw the chain across the latch to secure it again. She even glanced for a moment at the decorative table she had by the door for her tote bag. But the marble top alone weighed fifty pounds. There was no way she was going to be able to get that thing to slide to the front door.

A small meow greeted her as Mochi padded down the hall as if nothing in the world had changed.

"Come here sweet girl." Colleen crooned and dropped her bag and scooped up the cat.

Mochi purred softly, happy for once with the attention and curled up against Colleen's chest.

Slowly she made her way through the apartment, wandering, unsure of what to do with herself next.

She grabbed the remote off the arm of the couch and clicked on the T.V. wanting a noise outside of her own racing thoughts.

She had been too busy watching out for the world around her on the walk home she hadn't allowed herself to think deeply about the events of the day. Now alone, her mind wouldn't stop.

She had been held up at knife point. She Colleen Scott had actually been held up and robbed at knife point... and she wasn't quite sure how she felt about it. Her adrenaline had been going nonstop ever since she first saw his tall shadow behind her. Even now her heart still beat a little faster than she thought it had before.

What would have happened if she had refused him? Would he have simply fled, and left the store unharmed? Or would he have used that knife, killed her and possibly Roger too?

Colleen wandered aimlessly around her apartment until dusk began to fall. After the first twenty minutes Mochi had grown tired of the affection and had leapt from her arms, staying in the room only out of hope of getting a little treat.

When she realized that would not happen and that her owner seemed content to walk small circles around the rooms, lost in thought she stalked back to one of the large window sills that looked out over the city and curled up and fell asleep.

It was only the constant rumbling of Colleen's stomach that eventually broke her trance and focused her on a task of foraging her cupboards for dinner. With a box of Lucky Charms, that were only slightly stale, Colleen sat on the edge of her couch and watched as the evening news began.

The weather played; rain showers were expected through the weekend. Typical spring in New York. After the weather a "Top Breaking Story" Flashed across the screen and the evening anchors appeared seated behind their big news desk.

"Another armed robbery happened this afternoon this time hitting Campbells Jewelry. An iconic family-owned staple in the diamond district. Police reports show a long-time female employee was ambushed and held at knife point and was forced to empty out several cases of high-end jewelry before being tied up and left in the store as the man escaped. The store owner's son gave NEWS FIVE an exclusive stating 'everything of true value, our employee Colleen and my father are safe. The jewels were insured and will be far easier to replace.' Police chief Todd also speaking to NEWS FIVE urging businesses to tighten security and if anyone out there knows any information regarding the robberies to call the number on the screen or dial 911."

Colleen couldn't believe David had talked to the news already and used her name in his stupid interview. As if he really cared what happened to her. More so, she was surprised that she was so shocked about his douche bag behavior. Of course, David would already be contacting news outlets, he would try to get as much attention out of this as he could.

Colleen blankly watched the rest of the evening news, not really caring about the celebrity gossip or the chef they had on showing the best salads for spring. She ate her cereal in handfuls until her stomach finally stopped grumbling. She hoped someone checked the microwave and threw her leftover Lo-Mein out before it started to stink. She thought for a second about texting Roger, but her phone was still in her bag by the door and she was not motivated enough to go grab it.

Eventually Colleen grew tired and went to get ready for bed. She washed her face, staring at her eyes in the mirror. Surrounded by soap they had a bewildered appearance to them. She could see the fear from the day still reflecting back. She rinsed off and slipped under the covers, the bright city lights illuminating her bedroom. Mochi leaped softly on the bed, padding past her normal space on the empty side of the bed and curled up against Colleen. Her small weight giving an extra comfort and letting Colleen finally drift off to sleep.

Chapter Seven

Flashes of bright blue eyes swathed in mysterious black fabric drifted through Colleens dreams. It was the flash of a knife and a loud chime that shot her awake. Mochi yowled in aggravation at the sudden wake up.

The loud chime echoed again. Colleen's cellphone was ringing out in the living room where she had left it.

Groggily she padded across the apartment and fished the ringing phone from her bag. *Mom* flashed across the screen. She hadn't told her parents what had happened, but she knew her mom monitored the New York news like a hawk every morning and had probably seen David's interview.

"Hello." Colleen said after sliding the screen to answer.

"Collen! Are you okay, what happened? Your father and I are worried sick! We've been calling all morning; we saw the news!" Her mom screeched into the phone, not letting Colleen answer between questions.

"Mom!" Colleen finally interrupted. "I'm fine, yes, the store was robbed, but I'm fine. They got some jewelry and left."

"Oh Colleen! I knew moving to New York was a bad idea. Your father and I can be in the car in an hour and help move you right back home."

"Mom." Colleen gritted her teeth, the emotions from yesterday threatening to come out at her mother in unfiltered anger over the same argument they have every few months. "I am not moving back; this is the first thing that has happened in the seven years I have been here. And it can happen in Kentucky too."

"I just don't know..." Colleen heard her father grumbling in the background. "I agree with your father, maybe you should look at getting a job somewhere a little safer, maybe Macy's. They have a jewelry counter. And it's in the middle of the store, no one would be dumb enough to hold someone up at knife point in the middle of a Macy's."

Colleen rolled her eyes at her mom's naivety. In New York you could get held up anywhere.

"Mom. I am fine. Roger gave me the weekend off; I am going to rest and be back to work Monday."

Her mom chattered some more and Colleen listened and set her at ease while filling Mochi's food bowl. When she got her mom off the phone all remnants of the dreams had faded. But a headache had replaced them. She quickly got dressed in jeans and a thin pullover, throwing her hair up in a messy ponytail before walking out the door to find coffee. Carlos was quieter than normal as he prepared her drink. She assumed he had seen the news. As he reached for the normal To-Go cup Collen asked him if she could have it for in house. She never took time to sit and enjoy her drink, and she felt the urge to do so this morning rather than go directly back to her apartment and drink it alone. He gave her a sad smile as handed her a cup and saucer. A small chocolate chip scone was balanced on the end as well.

She took her breakfast over to a short bistro style table by the window and watched the people walk by as she sipped her latte. The welcome bell chimed and Colleen looked over as a tall blonde man wearing a black pea coat walked in. He placed an order with Carlos and lounged against the wall to wait, scrolling on his phone. His jaw was chiseled and his hair had just enough length to it that it flipped down, covering his eyes as he looked down.

He must have felt her stare as he looked up and met her gaze. Colleen quickly looked down at her mug, a little shocked at the deep blue eyes that had looked at her. She mentally shook herself the minute she did it though, she couldn't be scared at every set of blue eyes she saw.

There were a few other patrons in the shop, but the morning coffee rush was over. Colleen heard the footsteps near her and she looked up as the chair at the table next to her was pulled out and the blue-eyed man sat down. He caught her gaze again and smiled at her as he took a drink from his cup.

"Good morning." He said, pulling his phone back out of his pocket and reading something that flashed on the screen.

"Morning." Colleen murmured back to him. She tried to focus back on the people walking around outside in between taking bites of her scone.

"I've never been in here before; this place is nice." The man said putting his phone on the table and looking at Colleen over his cup as he took another drink.

"Oh yeah, it is. Carlos makes great drinks." She wasn't sure if it was what happened yesterday that was making her uneasy, or if it was the guy. But Colleen felt awkward trying to converse with the man.

"I just moved into the neighborhood and am still trying all of the local places, but I think this is my new favorite coffee shop. Do you usually come in here?" The man didn't look sketchy. He looked like the typical business man you'd see walking around New York. He had on a light grey suit that from what Colleen could see under the coat was well tailored, same with the white shirt that peaked out under the layers. Colleen could see his muscles pulling the fabric taught across his chest. His phone buzzed on the table but this time he ignored it, looking instead at Colleen.

"I come here every morning." Colleen started, kicking herself as she remembered this man was a stranger. "But uh, I usually take it to go and drink it on my way to work." She broke the eye contact he had been holding her in and stared down at her half empty cup.

"I see." The guy said, "too bad, it would have been fun to have company in the morning before work. I'm Brock by the way." He reached a hand out to her.

"Colleen." She took his hand, his grip firm but still careful with her much smaller hand.

"Nice to meet you, Colleen. You live in New York long?"

"I moved here seven years ago." Their hands were still linked across the walk way between the tables.

"Oh nice, I just got here few months ago. I'm originally from the west coast, so this has been a bit of a culture shock." His phone buzzed and buzzed as a call came through. "Excuse me." He said finally releasing her hand and answering the phone. He just listened to the person on the other end, who had apparently started talking the moment he answered. "I'll meet you in ten." He said in response to whatever the person on the other end of the call said before hanging up.

"Well work calls, of course."

"Of course." Colleen said with a small smile.

"Do you think I could maybe get your number? Maybe we can talk some more over dinner." Butterflies flew through Colleen's stomach.

"Um, yeah that would be nice." Colleen recited her phone number which he punched into his phone. Colleen felt her own phone vibrate in her jeans pocket. She pulled it out and saw a text from an unknown number. The text was just the emoji of a coffee cup and a winky face.

"There, now you have my number too. I'll text you later and arrange dinner." Brock stood and downed the rest of his drink before taking his cup over to the used bin by the counter. He turned back before walking out the door and winked at her.

Colleen watched him out the window as he walked away down the sidewalk. She hadn't even realized she was leaning to get one last look until her forehead bumped against the glass. She looked around embarrassed and hoping no one else noticed. There were only two other patrons left besides her in the shop. Neither of them paying her any attention.

Colleen finished her now cold coffee trying to process the last few days of her life. She couldn't believe it, yesterday she was held at knife point, and today she made a date. She slowly brought her cup over to the bin, and made her short walk back to the apartment, unsure if she should laugh or cry.

Chapter Eight

Heart still fluttering, she wasn't sure if it was from the robbery or the handsome stranger she'd just met. Mochi looked disgruntled when Colleen came back home mid-morning. She was used to napping alone on the couch, and was quite upset when Colleen sat next to her and turned on the TV. The news was replaying David's interview from last night. The anchor after reminded people that if they had any information on the suspects behind the string of robberies to call the police and let them know.

What are the odds? Colleen thought that the worse day of her life would have led to meeting her handsome coffee date. If it hadn't been for the robbery, she would have ordered her normal coffee to-go and would have been at work by the time Brock strolled in to the café, and they would have never met. Maybe this was the universe's way of apologizing for yesterday's scare.

Her phone dinged in her pocket, and a text from Brock flashed across her screen when she fished it out.

"It was great meeting you this morning. Would it be too soon to ask you to dinner tonight?"

The butterflies that had been fluttering in her chest as she read the message began to turn to stones that settled in her gut as a sense of guilt started to overwhelm her. Should she really be going out? She was given time off to work out what had happened to her, to process being tied up with a knife to her back. Should she really be going out with a guy she just met? Although after she met Brock, she had been able to walk back to her apartment without looking over her shoulder and fearing that a man in a dark sweatshirt and mask might be following her. And Colleen didn't want to feel like a prisoner in her home. Yes, the bad guy was still out there. And yes, it was completely possible a bad thing could happen to her again. But bad things could happen at any time. Shit, it was just a month ago she saw a lady almost get taken out by a taxi while in the crosswalk. So why should it matter what her timeline was for moving on.

It was great meeting you too. I would love to go out to dinner with you tonight.

Colleen texted back. She threw her hands against her mouth and screeched. She couldn't believe she was doing it. Maybe this was just an effect of the leftover adrenaline, but even if it was Colleen was going to ride it out until she crashed.

The rest of the day flew by. With her new energy from the excitement for her date, she deep cleaned her entire apartment, even opening the windows to allow some fresh air in. To finish it off she lit a candle before deciding to jump in the shower. Throughout it all she also was busy sharing cute flirty texts back and forth with Brock. Nothing to deep, she wanted to save a lot of the 'get to know you' questions for dinner. He had picked out a small bistro that was a block from the coffee shop. He said he had met a business partner there one of his first nights in the city and loved it. Colleen had seen it a few times. It was actually a place she had asked her ex to take her to a few times, but he had been a comic book artist who didn't really ever have steady work and was worried about the menu price and they never went.

Working in the fashion industry, she was familiar with men's attire. She especially could tell the difference between an expensive suit that was tailored to fit, and a cheap imitation that wore the man more than the man wore it. Brock's suit had certainly been tailored. From the flashes she got when his coat moved when he walked, she could see that the fabric had clung perfect to his body, hugging him well while still being professional. The light grey has also complimented his sandy blonde hair perfectly. That paired with the choice of restaurant told Colleen that he had great taste. A refreshing change from the men who she had dated previously, though Colleen knew also from experience at her job that money couldn't buy class.

Standing in her robe with the towel wrapped around her hair Colleen pulled dress after dress out of her closet, trying to find one that wasn't so "work appropriate". Finally, she found a sleek black shin length dress that had a fun handkerchief design to the hem, small cream beading and thin straps. It was fun and flirty but also dressy enough to guarantee she would adhere to any dress code the restaurant might have.

Brock had texted earlier, asking if she wanted him to pick her up on his way. Colleen might have been taking a risk with going out with a guy she had just met that morning, but she wasn't dumb. She'd had one knife to her throat already this week, she really didn't need to risk someone actually murdering her. Colleen had held her breath when texting him back that she'd just meet him there, worried he would think she was being evasive. But she was relieved when he didn't seem offended and said he would meet her out front at seven.

She dried her heir straight and left it down, letting it fall over her shoulders. Colleen finished her outfit with a simple snake chain necklace and diamond studs. She also gave her dress a good lint roll to remove the hair Mochi left after her approving body rub before meeting her ordered cab outside.

Chapter Nine

The restaurant was beautifully lit when she pulled up. The sun had already set and the accented black iron lanterns attached to the dark brick was giving a warm inviting glow to the sidewalk. Brock was waiting as promised just outside the door. He met the cab as it pulled up to the curb and opened the door for Colleen, offering her a hand as well to hold as she stepped out.

"Wow." He said as she stood next to him. "You look absolutely exquisite."

Colleen felt her cheeks flush at the compliment. "Thank you. You look pretty nice yourself."

And he did. He had changed from his earlier business attire and was wearing a dark navy button-down shirt that was tucked into black jeans. He had a watch on that to Colleen looked like a Rolex, but she couldn't quite catch a good look at the face to confirm if it was authentic or not.

"Thank you." He flashed a grin that caused a small dimple to appear on his right cheek.

"Shall we." He gestured to the large wooden door to the restaurant. Colleen matched his grin and tucked her hair behind her ear and followed him in. He held the door open for her, and she could feel his gaze behind her and she smiled knowing he was taking in the full view of how the dress hugged her curves as she walked, her heels exaggerating her natural hip sway a little more than normal.

Brock had made a reservation so they got seated right away. The maître d took them to a small private table over in a corner. The restaurant wasn't large. And it spaced its tables out enough to allow private conversations and give a more intimate feel. The inside was lit by lanterns similar to the ones outside, giving a warm glow to the dark wooden tables.

Their waiter brought them a wine list and they each ordered a glass of merlot. He went to grab them while the pair looked over the menu. Colleen worked in the luxury industry so she was used to looking at high priced items, but even she was surprised at the prices on the menu. The roasted chicken with seasonal vegetables alone was sixty dollars. She did a quick glance over the top of her menu at Brock. He didn't seem nervous or uneasy. And she reminded herself he had been here before, so he had to know these prices before choosing the place. He was looking over the menu and didn't seem to notice her stare. At the angle he was reading the menu she was able to get a better look at the watch, it indeed said Rolex. It appeared to be a *Date Just* with the platinum face. A nice watch if it was indeed genuine.

"Do you like Rolex?" He asked. She hadn't noticed she was staring so intently at his watch. Her cheeks flushed embarrassed. She didn't want him to think she was vain.

"Oh, um yeah, I do. I actually work at a small local store in the diamond district. We don't sell Rolex but I've cleaned plenty of them to admire."

"Do you like your job?" He asked placing his menu down on the table.

"I do, I really enjoy being a part of people's special moments. A lot are signified with jewelry, and they all get stories to go with."

Colleen lowered her menu as Brock stared thoughtfully for a moment.

"I never thought about it that way. That would be fun to be a part of. You work in jewelry, so you must have you heard of the robberies going on huh?"

Colleen felt a knot form in her chest. Thankfully the waiter came back, placing two glasses of wine on the table and asking if they were ready to order.

"Ladies first." Brock said gesturing his hand to her.

Colleen forgot she was supposed to be looking at the menu in her hands. She quickly picked the first thing her eyes landed on which happened to be the Greek sliders. Not something she normally would have picked, but it sounded good enough. The waiter smiled and took her menu before turning to Brock.

He ordered a steak, rare. And a bread basket for the table.

As the waiter walked away, he turned his attention back to her, clearly picking the conversation back up where they had left it.

"Yes, actually our store was robbed yesterday." Brock's face was shocked at her answer.

"Oh wow, I'm sorry I brought it up." His smile dropped, and he looked down at his hands, seeming to be ashamed to make eye contact with her now. But Colleen didn't want to spoil the mood of their evening before it even began.

"It's okay, it's been all over the news so it's a natural question. It happened, and we are all fine now. Luckily the store has good insurance so we will be able to pick up and move on from this." She felt her tension release when he also seemed to relax. But she definitely wanted to move the conversation away from the current topic.

"So, what do you do?"

The waiter came with their bread basket and a small plate with butter.

"Thank you." They said in unison as the waiter smiled and walked away.

"I work in the finance district." He answered reaching for a roll and cutting it open with his butter knife. "I help manage corporate accounts for our company. It's actually really boring work, but it pays better than my old job and has a much more flexible schedule."

Colleen spread butter on her own roll and took a bite. The bread was still warm and soft. The butter was also incredibly rich and smooth, she wondered if they made it in house.

"Good, isn't it?" Brock asked chuckling at her and popping a piece of his into his mouth.

"So good!" Colleen also laughed and took another bite.

"Just wait till the meal gets here, you'll see why I suggested this place."

"I can't wait." Colleen grinned at Brock and took a sip from her wine glass. She couldn't remember the last time she had enjoyed someone's company as much as she was.

He grinned back at her and raised his glass towards her.

"Too chance meetings."

Colleen raised her glass and gently clinked it against his.

"To chance meetings."

Chapter Ten

Their dinner flew by. Colleen couldn't remember the last time she had such an amazing first date. Brock was interesting and funny, and loved to answer her questions as well as ask his own. She knew he was born in Arizona but moved to California for college and worked there until his current job offered to move him to New York. He was an only child, both his parents had passed a few years ago. He was also older than her by a few years, but Colleen liked that.

He had been right, the food was phenomenal. Her sliders had perfect flavor and just the right amount of sauce. Brock's steak had looked amazing too. He barely had to use his knife to cut it, and the bite he fed her off his fork had been delicious. She may have flirted a bit in pulling the bite gently off with her teeth. And the way his eyes flickered with heat while he watched made her feel that he was really liking her as well.

Upon Brocks insistence they each ordered a slice of the chocolate cake as well. Which again, he had been right, even though she was full from dinner, she ate every last piece of the decadent cake.

Colleen was a little bummed when the waiter came and cleared their dishes and dropped off the check. Brock pulled his Amex out of his wallet and paid the waiter. He pulled a fifty-dollar bill from his wallet and placed it on the table as a tip before helping her out of her chair.

He placed a hand gently against her lower back and walked just behind her through the restaurant, the touch sending tingles of excitement racing down her spine to her toes.

The air outside had cooled off slightly during dinner and Colleen wished she had brought a shall with her. Goose bumps raised on her arms. Brock waved for a cab that was parked at the corner. It slowly pulled up.

"I had a great time tonight." He said turning and looking at Colleen.

"I did too, this was the most fun I have had in a long time." She had that anxious anticipation that she got whenever she got to the end of first dates. *What would he do? Would he go in for the kiss? A hug. Oh god.* She thought, *would he shake her hand?*

Colleen was trapped in her thoughts as the cab pulled up right in front of them. Brock opened the door for her and she thought for sure he wasn't even going to try to shake her hand when she went to pass him. Until she felt his hand slide along her hip and stop her. He pulled her towards him and used his other hand to gently lift her chin. His blue eyes had an intensity in them that instantly made her insides melt. He bent his head down and Colleen felt her eyes drift closed as he pressed his mouth against hers. His lips were firm against hers, and he tasted like wine and chocolate. He was soft at first but there seemed to be a spark of electricity that flashed between them. She stepped closer, pressing her body against his. His chest was muscled and hard under her hands as she slowly slid them up over his shoulders.

His hand also drifted up from her chin to the back of her head, tangling in her hair as her pressed against her. The cab driver disappeared from both their minds and it was only when another cab behind them honked his horn did they slowly pull apart.

"I think this is good night." Brock whispered breathlessly.

"Or you could come back to my place." Colleen heard herself say. She had never brought a man back to her place on the first date. But this was a week of first apparently and maybe she was still riding the adrenaline high but this first she knew would be a good one.

She slid into the cab and watched as he slid in beside her. She rattled off her address to the cab driver. Brocks fingers intertwined with hers and he leaned over and brushed soft tantalizing kisses against her neck the whole drive home.

Chapter Eleven

Colleen cursed the two red lights the cab had to stop at on the drive back to her apartment. Brock's attention to her neck was causing her to ignite inside and she needed to get him home... now.

When they finally pulled up out front Brock quickly paid the cab driver and then grabbed her hand. She led him up to her apartment and they had barely made it in the door before she turned and reached for him.

And he was right there with her. Their mouths met, forming and moving together. He seemed eager to touch her anywhere and everywhere. His tongue slipped into her mouth, exploring and Colleen choked back a moan.

She backed them slowly into her bedroom, desperate to get him in her bed. As soon as she felt the rug under foot she was kicking out of her shoes, not breaking her mouth from his. His hand roamed to her back, grabbing the zipper of her dress. He had it unzipped in one smooth movement. With his hands already there he unlatched her strapless bra and tossed it across the room. He broke their kiss long enough to look at her. He seemed to be drinking her in with his eyes, gazing at her breasts like a starving man looking at food for the first time in days.

Colleen decided it was unfair that Brock was still fully clothed. She reached for his chest and began working on the buttons. Pulling his mouth back to hers as she did so. He helped shrug out of it and exposed his broad muscled chest. Colleen raked her hands over the skin, loving the feeling of him under her. She quickly reached down and undid his pants. As soon as he stepped out of them, he leaned and scooped her into his arms. He kissed her throat and she leaned her head back and moaned as he layed her on the bed.

Her curtains were still open, so she was able to see him in the city lights that came through. He reminded her of the statues of Adonis she saw in the Met. Every part of him seemed sculpted and designed by the gods. He too seemed to be admiring what he saw. The evidence apparent between his legs. He leaned in and kissed her again, using his tongue to plunge in and out of her mouth in a promise.

"Wait, one second." Colleen gasped out. Brock pulled away, his face puzzled. Colleen leaned over to her night stand and pulled one of the emergency condoms she kept in it and tossed it to Brock. He caught it and smiled devilishly at her as he slowly ripped the wrapper open with his teeth. Colleen caught herself biting her lip as she watched him roll the condom on. He then slowly crawled forward and sucked her lip from between her teeth and bit it gently. He then moved from her mouth, down her chin and back to her throat, nipping lightly as he went. But his excursion didn't end there. He made his way slowly down to her breasts. First pulling one into his mouth, then the other. Colleen gasped, grabbing his thick blonde hair in her hands. He slowly pulled her thong away, and threw it across the room.

"Oh god Colleen," he said with a ragged breath, "you're so beautiful." His hands slowly slid up her legs.

"Please don't stop." Colleen moaned, missing his mouth on her. He obliged, quickly ducking down between her legs. She felt his hands gently push her legs farther apart before the punch of heat from his mouth taking her.

"Oh god!" Colleen yelled out as his tongue licked up her core. He took his time, driving her right to the edge before pulling back and planting a kiss to each thigh.

"Brock." She whimpered. "I need you inside me." She arched up grabbing at his shoulders and pulling him up back to her mouth. She could taste herself on his tongue, which only intensified Colleen's need. As he crushed his mouth to hers, he settled between her legs and pushed inside her slowly. Colleen moaned as she felt the first bit of him enter her.

His cock was bigger than any she had ever had and he stretched her in a way that was sending her spiraling. He paused, letting her adjust. He then pulled out and plunged back in a little farther, and farther until he was fully seated.

He moaned her name as she pushed her hips up to meet him fully. He then set a slow methodical pace, swiveling his hips into her. She could feel ever bit of him press up against her. She stared into his blue eyes, seeing the raw heat in them. She memorized them, letting those blue eyes burn away the memory of the ones that had haunted her dreams the night before.

Colleen knew she was getting close; her body was right on the edge. Brock seemed to sense it too as his pace began to increase. Her breath came out in gasps as he plunged in and out. It was when he then brought his hand down between them and began rubbing her clit that she felt herself erupt. And as she climaxed, she felt him meet her, shouting her name and bracing his hands on either side of her, keeping himself from falling on top of her.

Brock's chest was heaving as he slowly pulled out of her with a groan. He rolled onto his back next to her. Colleen couldn't even tell if she was back in her own body yet. She had never had sex like that before.

She turned her head and looked over at the man laying next her.

"That was amazing." She whispered.

His face broke out into a big smile, that little dimple becoming even more prominent. He reached over and grabbed a strand of her hair and twirled it around his finger.

"Yeah, that was. Tell me what you're thinking." He continued playing with her hair.

"I'm thinking I want to ask you to stay, but I don't want to scare you and think I'm needy." She looked from his fingers to his face as his twirling stilled.

"I would love to stay." He propped himself up and leaned over her pressing her into the pillows, his chest pushing against her breasts. He pressed his mouth against hers, and they melded into the night.

Chapter Twelve

When Colleen woke up in the morning there was a soft, but persistent weight pushing against her rib cage. She opened her eyes and saw Mochi standing on her chest and staring at her with slitted agitated eyes. It was clearly later in the morning than Colleen normally woke up, causing someone's breakfast to be late.

Colleen shifted up, earning a sharp stab in the skin from tiny claws before Mochi jumped to the floor. The bed was empty, and the apartment was quiet. Colleen stood and walked out, no sign of men's clothes or presence left. The only evidence of last nights events was a sweet soreness between her legs which was now causing a knot to form in her stomach.

"Of course, he didn't stay." She mumbled to herself while scooping dry cat food into the bowl. Mochi already grabbing pieces as they fell and eating it like she hadn't been fed in days. As Colleen moved towards the bathroom in hopes of showering off the feeling of regret a small knock sounded at the door. She grabbed her robe off the hook in her bedroom, securing the sash as she peeked out the peep hole to see who could be at her door. Shocked Colleen opened the door and saw Brock standing on her little welcome mat in last night's clothes, holding two coffees and a paper pastry bag in his hands.

"Good morning." He said with his handsome half smile.

"Good morning." Colleen said, still shocked by him showing back up.

"Sorry I left, I was going to make coffee, but you don't have a coffee pot. So, I ran down to the café we met at and grabbed some breakfast." He held the goodies in his hands up a little higher, angling the cup in his right hand towards her a little more. Indicating that one as hers. She accepted it, shifting to the side to let him back in.

"Thank you." She took a sip; it was a cinnamon latte and the perfect temperature. She could smell the pastries as her walked past her too, her stomach growling.

He placed the bag on the counter and pulled out two large bear claws, handing one to her.

"Who doesn't have a coffee maker?" He gestured to her near bare counters. Aside from Mochis food and water fountain there was a knife block with three mismatched knives, a small vase with fake flowers she had gotten at a thrift store and a small hand towel next to some scented soap.

"I don't really cook in the kitchen. It's mostly for snacks, leftover takeout and wine." Colleen shrugged and took a bite of the bear claw. It had a sweet glaze and chunks of apple.

"I wouldn't call making coffee 'cooking'." Brock chuckled and sipped his coffee, having devoured his pastry in three bites.

"I just never felt the need, Carlos just makes it better." Colleen shrugged and slowly finished her own breakfast.

"He does make a great cup of coffee; I will admit to that." He cheered his cup towards her and took another drink.

Colleen's fingers were sticky from the pastry, she moved towards the sink to wash her hands when Brock caught her by the wrist. Slowly he moved her fingers to his mouth and gently pulled the tip of one finger into his mouth. Colleen gasped slightly as his tongue lavished her pointer finger before moving onto the middle, and then the ring. As he finished his 'cleaning' he gently pulled her close to him, loosening the sash around her waist as he did.

When her robe dropped to the ground he leaned back, admiring her body under the lights of the kitchen.

Quickly he grabbed her by the waist and lifted her onto the counter.

"Well, your ample counter space is good for one thing." He gave her a rogue smile as he bent over her and kissed her hard.

His tongue plunging into her mouth and twisting like it did with her fingers. As he did that his hands slowly traced up her legs, his fingers gentle and light.

He pulled back, his eyes dark with need as he dropped to his knees, spreading her legs wide against the counter.

"I am going to watch you come undone for me." He growled before putting his mouth between her legs. His tongue plunged inside her and Colleen bit back a scream. She hadn't realized how ready she was for him. She threw her head back, thankful for the counter size for the first time since she moved in. He slowly pulled his tongue back out.

"I want you to watch me, I want to see your face." Brock commanded, Colleen used her elbows to prop herself up and she stared directly into his eyes and had to fight falling back again as he slowly drew his tongue up her center.

"You are so beautiful." He whispered and used his fingers to spread her wider open, giving himself more access.

Every part of Colleen was shaking, her arms as they tried to keep her up, her legs which were draped over Brocks wide shoulders.

His deep blue eyes never left her face. It was when he pushed two fingers inside her that he got what he had wanted and watch her come apart around him.

She couldn't fight the scream back this time as she came around his fingers, her arms finally giving out.

Quickly Brock stood, gently putting her legs on the ground. He grabbed her waist and flipped her, using his feet to push hers farther apart. He bent over and whispered in a tone that she could only describe as animalistic "My turn."

She heard the rip of another condom wrapper and then he sound of his zipper as he freed himself from his pants and it was just a breath later he shoved himself inside her.

"Oh fuck!" Colleen screamed, her body absorbing him easily in one push thanks to her climax.

"Oh god you feel good." He grabbed a handful of her hair in one hand and gave it a soft pull back as he slid out and slammed himself back in. Colleen gasped again in pleasure. He set a hard pace and it wasn't long until Colleen came for the second time, Brock joining her a second later.

"Are you okay?" Brock finally asked after a moment. He gently brushed Colleen's hair from her face. She smiled at him, loving the gentleness he showed her.

"Yes, I'm fine. That was definitely a good use for the counter space. Glad I don't have a coffee maker now?"

"Very." He smiled wide. "I have a meeting at ten this morning, and I am going to have to stop by my place to shower and change so I should probably head out here soon. But do you have plans tomorrow?" Brock stood up, pulling Colleen into his arms.

"I'm free all day tomorrow."

He bent down and kissed her softly. "Not anymore you're not."

Chapter Thirteen

Brock left shortly after their little sexcapade in the kitchen. Colleen showered herself off and got dressed in jeans and a sweater unsure of how to spend her rare free Saturday.

After pacing restlessly between her couch and bedroom Colleen finally grabbed her purse and left the apartment deciding to head down to some of her favorite local thrift shops in the neighborhood.

The first one she stopped at was higher end, known for preowned designer purses and clothes. It was one of Colleen's favorite places to grab work clothes. Why buy a new Gucci blazer for almost four grand when you can pick up last seasons that was worn once by a fabulous Manhattan socialite for less than a quarter of the price.

Colleen wandered through the racks leisurely looking at the blouses when she felt her phone buzz in her pocket.

Heading into another meeting, how's your morning been?

Colleen smiled at the little check in.

It's been good, just out here boosting the economy.

She snapped a selfie in the store and sent it with her reply. Within moments of it being sent a small heart reaction reply came through as his response. Tucking her phone back into her jeans pocket she finished her browse of the store, contrary to her text she left without buying anything. Unfortunately, they were between the season change over so there wasn't anything new since the last time she had been in.

Going back out to the sidewalk the city was bustling. Workers were out on lunch, people with the days off like her were out doing their weekend shopping causing the sidewalk to feel more congested.

After a few more stores and securing a new skirt set Colleen decided it was time to grab some lunch and head back home.

She had peaked at her phone a few times throughout the day checking for anymore texts, but Brock must still be busy in his meetings. She slipped it into her purse after the last time checking it, convincing herself she was getting overly fixated on it over a man she had gone out with once. Even if she had slept with him also twice now.

Colleen grabbed a sub from the deli a street over from her house. As she made her way around the corner, she got an odd feeling of someone watching her. The small hairs on the back of her neck stood up, and she turned and saw a man in all black a few paces behind her.

He had a ball cap on and his head was turned down towards the phone in his hand, but Colleen still felt like his attention was on her and not the device. Turning back around she quickened her pace, feeling a sense of de ja vu to the afternoon after the robbery when she also had a man in a baseball cap she felt was following her.

She fought the urge to keep looking back, instead focusing on getting to her building.

When she did make it to the door of her building, she ducked through it and then scooted over against the inside wall, her heart pounding in her ears. She gripped the bags in her hand tightly, prepared to use them as weapons if the man in black followed her inside the building. As she ground her teeth she looked back out in his direction, and saw no one dressed all in black amongst the people left on the sidewalk. He was gone.

Colleen looked around, making sure she hadn't missed him, or that he wasn't hiding in the crowd. A few people gave her an odd look as they walked past.

Quickly Colleen walked back into her building. As soon as her feet hit the stairs she broke out into a run, taking them two at a time until she hit her floor. She still didn't stop until she was in her apartment and the door was locked.

Her chest heaving, she dropped her purse and shopping bag in the entry and strode to the bathroom. Colleen gripped the sink with both hands, her breath coming in and out in quick gasps and looked at her reflection.

Her eyes were wide and full of fear, her skin flush and she could swear she could see her heart beating in her throat. Colleen swallowed hard, trying to stop the sick feeling creeping through her.

She slowly sank to the floor, the cool tile feeling nice against her heated skin. She had never had a panic attack before, but she was pretty sure this was what one felt like.

Colleen wasn't sure how long she lay there on the bathroom floor. Mochi had swished in and out when she didn't get any attention. And she thought a few times she had heard her cell phone ring, though the sound was muffled by her purse and the distance from the bathroom. Still Colleen laid there. What was she going to do? She thought. She couldn't breakdown every time she saw a man dressed in black. This was New York, half the population only wore black. Her stomach growled, and she remembered her sandwich that lay forgotten on the floor. She was sure the tuna fish in it was not fit to be eaten anymore from sitting at room temperature for so long.

Colleen was just starting to think about what she should do next now that her breathing and heart rate had slowed when she heard a quiet knock at the door. She didn't move, she wasn't sure yet if she was capable of getting up. After a few more moments Colleen heard the sound of the front door sweep open and a familiar male voice call out her name.

Brock. But how had he gotten in? Colleen tried to think back to if she had locked her door when she got home. She could have sworn she had, but then again, she hadn't been in her normal mental state, so maybe she had forgotten. But still, why was he here?

"Colleen!" he yelled a little louder, probably growing concerned over the mess of forgotten food and bags in her entry.

She heard footsteps quickly echo through the apartment and turned her head just in time to see him round the corner in her bedroom and spy her on the floor.

"Oh my god! Colleen are you okay? What happened?" He knelt beside her, his hands gently sweeping hair from her face. His thumb grazed her cheek, brushing tears. She hadn't even realized she had been crying.

"I'm okay." Colleen croaked out. "It's nothing."

"What do you mean it's nothing? Your sitting crying on the bathroom floor. What happened? Are you hurt?" His eyes raked over her, looking for a physical sign of distress.

She shook her head, and reached up to rub her eyes.

"It's just a panic attack, I think."

His body relaxed a little, but his face remained worried.

"Here let's get you up off the floor, okay?" He waited for her nod before gently scooping her up in his arms and carried her over to the bed. He laid her onto her back and sat on the edge next to her.

"Do you want to talk about it?" He grabbed one of her hands, his thumb brushing soft circles.

"It's so stupid, I saw a guy in black walking behind me on my way home. I thought he was following me, he remind-ed me of the guy who robbed the store. He wasn't though.

Which is why this is so stupid. But I don't know, once the fear set in, I couldn't stop it." Just remembering it had Colleen's heart rate picking up again.

"It's not stupid." Brock said, his face softening. "It only happened a few days ago. It's going to take some time to feel safe again."

Colleen nodded, feeling better now that she was off the floor and Brock was there. Which reminded her.

"How did you know something was wrong? And how did you get in? I could have sworn I locked the door."

"I had been texting you, but it showed you hadn't read the messages. So, I tried calling. When you didn't answer I just had a feeling. I knocked a few times and then tried the door knob; it opened right up." His worried expression tugged at something in Colleen's chest.

"Weird, I could have sworn I locked it." Colleen shifted and propped her head up with one of her arms.

"I can take a look at it if you'd like. Maybe it's a faulty lock."

"Good with money, rescuing damsels in distress, and a handyman, how on earth are you still single?" Colleen asked, chuckling.

Brock laughed so hard he shook the bed.

"Guess I was just looking for the right damsel." His face had relaxed since her joke and Colleen couldn't help herself as she reached up and grabbed him, pulling him to her. He leaned forward, more than happy to oblige. She kissed him, feeling the last dregs of anxiety leave her as she did. He kissed back for a few moments and then pulled back when he heard the grumble from her stomach.

"Why don't I go grab some food and then we can take a look at that door?" He appraised her as he leaned back.

"That sounds good, I'll be okay." Brock leaned down and kissed her one more time before getting up and leaving the apartment.

A few moments after he left Colleen slowly got up from the bed and made her way to the entry to pick up her discarded items. She brought her purse and her new clothes into her room, discarding the sub in the trash on her way. She then made her way back to the front door and looked at the door knob. Curiously she turned the lock and tried to twist the door knob, it didn't budge. She slowly pulled her hand back and stared at the lock, had she simply imagined she had flipped it? Had she in her haste and fear forgot? She doubted it, but why would Brock lie? And how else would he have gotten in? She wrapped her arms around herself and slowly made her way to the living room.

She turned on the TV trying to shake the odd feeling about the door lock.

"Breaking this afternoon, another robbery took place. This time at another family-owned jewelry store located in the famous diamond district. Police telling us that thousands of dollars of merchandise were stolen, the thief once again using a knife to subdue the store clerk. Though no one was harmed this marks the fith robbery of this nature. Police are asking that if anyone has any tips or information to please call the number we have at the bottom of the screen."

When would they find who was doing this? Colleen thought, her heart going out to the clerk at the store who was now going to feel exactly what she had been for the past few days. She remembered the calm way the man had robbed them; he had been so in control. He hadn't worried about being caught, and after he had just disappeared into the crowd, as if he was any other person.

The news switched to sports by the time Brock knocked on the door again. This time Colleen got up and let him in, thought she was half tempted to make him try the door again now that she knew it was locked. But she was exhausted from the day and was ready to eat.

He had gone to a sushi place and had gotten an assortment of rolls to choose from.

Colleen unpacked everything onto the coffee table and they spent their evening lounging on the couch, watching random movies that were on cable and eating sushi. Mochi had even joined them, choosing to lay across Brock's lap as if in a sign of dominance. Instead, she became a purring puddle under his pets and sweet words about her being a pretty girl.

At some point Colleen fell asleep half way through one of the Marvel movies.

She woke for a moment when she felt strong arms lift her off the couch. She curled against Brock's chest as he carried her to the bedroom.

After laying her on the bed and pulling the blankets over her Brock leaned down and kissed the top of her head.

He moved as if to leave, Colleen reaching out and grabbed his arm.

"Stay with me?" She whispered.

"Alright." He whispered back. She heard him move to the other side of the bed and she rolled over when she felt his weight on the mattress. He wrapped one arm over her and she tucked against his chest. She fell asleep quickly, breathing in his scent.

Chapter Fouteen

Sunday went by like a dream. Brock had stayed with her the night before; he had gone home to change and when he came back, he had brought a small tool box and a brand-new door knob. He had fixed it for her while she played goalie, keeping Mochi in the apartment while the door was open. The small feline seemed to be under the impression life would be far better out in the hall.

They had ordered in lunch and spent the rest of the day talking and learning about each other.

Roger had called her that afternoon to check in, he planned on opening the store Monday morning and wanted to see if she was ready to come back. She told him she would absolutely see him the next morning, she was ready to move on. Brock had offered to walk with her on the way the next morning, but she knew it was something she was going to have to get back to doing on her own. He had respected her decision, but had made her promise to text him when she got there and when she got home.

Brock had insisted on finishing out their weekend by going out on to a 'proper meal' as he put it. Colleen had suggested a popular Italian place a few blocks away that served family style, she hadn't felt like dressing up and this place allowed casual. They had taxied there together and split the Lasagna that was big enough for each of them to have a to-go box for lunch the next day.

At the end of the night, he walked her to her door and kissed her goodnight letting her know he didn't plan on staying so that she was well rested for her return to work. However, the kiss definitely told her how much he wanted to stay.

But Monday morning came and she was glad she was by herself, and could get back into her morning routine.

She showered, dressed in her new skirt set she found, fed Mochi and gave her a few extra cuddles. Walked to the café where she chatted with Carlos, stalling her walk a bit.

Eventually she couldn't stall anymore and she made her way to the store. Her stride was slower than normal, giving herself time to look closely at the people around her, searching if anyone seemed to be following or paying her too much attention. Her heart picked up a few times when someone seemed to be going the same direction as her for too long. But soon enough she was standing out front of Campbells Jewelry, alone. The metal cage was down and locked tight, the lights dim inside. She pulled her phone out and shot a text to Brock.

At work safe and sound

She banged on the cage and watched Roger appear out of the back and walk towards her. She felt her phone buzz in her hand.

Have a great day, text me when you leave and get home

Colleen smiled at her phone as Roger lifted the metal cage.

"Good morning." She said trying not to sound as anxious as she felt.

"Good morning, Colleen, how are you feeling?" Roger snapped the lock of the cage back down, looking left and right at the people walking down the street.

"I'm doing okay, ready to be back at work." She could see the worry on his face.

"Well, I'm glad you're here. I spoke to David; I have hired a private security guard who will be here from open until we leave at night. I don't know why I never did before, ninety percent of the stores on the street have guards, even those clothing stores on the next street over do. That way we have an extra set of eyes to watch the place and he will be armed so that way people will think twice before trying to rob this place again."

Colleen felt the knot in her stomach loosen slightly, armed security would definitely prevent another incident.

"Of course, David thinks it's a ridiculous waste of money, especially when our insurance rates are going to raise now with the loss claim. But I don't agree with him on the likelihood of another robbery happening. I've also talked to him about coming in more too."

That part Colleen didn't like as much. She loved working with Roger, but David was a spoiled pompous ass she could do without.

Colleen and Roger got the store set up pretty quickly due to the lack of inventory. Colleen used the extra time to try to rearrange the cases to make the large loss of product not as noticeable. Five minutes before opening a man in black Kevlar with a security badge and a gun strapped to his waist nocked on the cage. Roger had let him in and gone through the store showing him the layout. When the store opened the guard who Colleen learned was named Clint took a position near the front door. The store was busy, but more so with people who were curious about the robbery. Thankfully when a couple of reporters had snuck in and tried to record a story Clint stepped in and escorted them off site.

"Just that alone made him worth the money." Roger had whispered to Colleen after Clint ushered the last reporter out to the sidewalk. The short man with the camera arguing that he had a right to film his story.

By the end of the day Colleen was exhausted. David had shown up and was irritated that his father hadn't allowed the news to come inside for reports and stories saying the press coverage was good for business. They had fought in the shop for several minutes before David had been banished back out to the sales floor.

Before leaving Colleen texted Brock to let him know. Her phone rang.

"Hello." She answered.

"Hey how was your first day back?" Brock's voice came through.

"It was good, busy. Roger hired an armed guard to watch the store from now on." Colleen began her walk home.

"Oh really? Did he use a company or hire privately?"

Colleen chuckled, typical guy question she decided "Privately. I'm not sure how Roger found him but he did a pretty good job today. We had some reporters come in and try getting stories. It was super annoying. But the guy had them out on the street before they could get much for a story."

"Well, that's good you guys got some extra security. Are you feeling better now that the day is over?" Brock's voice was calm and easy, relaxing her slightly with the commonality their conversations were getting. She liked it, being asked the simple "how was your day" after work.

"Yeah, I am. It was good to get back and be so busy, kind of took my mind off it after a bit." Colleen crossed the street with a crowd at the crosswalk, only a block from home now.

"So, what are your plans for the evening?"

"I'm probably just going to order in and take a bath. What about you?" Colleen had made it to her street. She heard voices behind Brock through the line.

"Well, I am stuck at work for a few more hours, I wish I was with you in the bath though." His voice was low, probably to keep the people around him from hearing. Colleen smiled;

her stomach fluttered at the memory of seeing him naked in her bed.

"I wish you were too."

"I'm going to be pretty tied up this week, maybe I can cook for you this weekend?"

"You cook too?" Colleen playfully gasped and tried to hide the shock in her voice.

Brock chuckled.

"Yes, I cook, and unfortunately my counters do have appliances for cooking on them, so we will have to find somewhere else to have fun."

"Bummer." Colleen mocked disappointment. She had made it to the front of her building and was heading up the stairs.

"Well, it sounds like your home now, so my work here is done and I will have to go back to the one that pays the bills."

"Work?" Colleen asked confused. It suddenly dawned on her that she had made it all the way back home without feeling or worrying about being followed. "Oh, that was tricky of you." She grumbled. As she made it to her front door there sat a surprise.

A large floral bouquet sat outside her door, it was a massive bloom of pink and green flowers. A small teddy bear sat next to it.

"What is this for?" She tucked the phone between her ear and shoulder and bent down to grab the gifts.

"I've heard its customary to give a girl flowers, and I figured I couldn't be there so I'd give you something to cuddle tonight as well. Although I selfishly hope you still miss me." She could hear the smile in his voice, but her toes curled at the low, growly tone he used at the end.

"I love it, thank you! And this little guy is cute, but I don't think you have anything to worry about." Colleen chuckled. She balanced the flowers and bear into the crook of her arm and fished her keys out. She opened her own new door knob and walked inside.

"Well, I'm glad you had such a good day, I hope you have a great night and I'll talk to you tomorrow." Brock said, the voices she could hear in the background through the line were getting a little louder so she assumed he was stepping into another meeting.

"Thank you for making my day even better. Have a great night." She kissed into the phone before hanging up.

She placed the flowers on the coffee table. She bent down and breathed in their scent, her toes curling in her shoes. She smiled all the way to the bedroom, tucking the bear against her pillow she went into the bathroom and started the water in her bath and imagined what a man like Brock's apartment would be like. She felt like she was in high school again, excited for her date this weekend.

Chapter Fifteen

That week had gone by in a blur of busy days at the store, secretly texting Brock in the back room between customers and phone calls on the way home.

By the time Saturday came around Colleen was so excited she felt a little silly. It had only been a little over a week since she met Brock, but she could tell she was falling hard for him.

It took her a few hours to get ready. She took a forty-minute shower, making sure to shave every inch on herself and scrubbing down with her favorite rose scented body scrub that had essential oils that allowed the scent to linger. She dressed in a satiny black dress with thin straps and stopped just above the knee with a small slit in the side that exposed her thigh when she sat down.

She wore her killer black strappy heels and underneath everything she wore the new black lacey lingerie she had bought Thursday after work.

Before leaving she left Mochi a second bowl of food for breakfast tomorrow.

Brock had sent her the address for his place and though he was really close to her apartment she chose to flag down a cab due to the height of her shoes and the skimpiness of her dress. She wasn't a fool to walk down a busy New York City street alone dressed like she was.

When the cab pulled up in front of the building Colleen gasped. She had seen this large building a few times, its brick was illuminated by giant ornate sconces and had a front door man. She had dreamed of living here but knew even with her decent commissions she'd never be able to afford it.

The doorman opened the large glass door to allow her in.

"Who are you visiting today madam?" the elderly gentle-man asked.

"Brock Dent. I believe he's in apartment 1215."

"Ah yes, Ms. Scott I presume. Mr. Dent let me know you were coming. Let me take you to the lift."

He guided her over to a large ornate elevator. The glass doors opened when the doorman scanned a security pad with a pass card. He waved his arm encouraging her to step inside. He leaned in and pressed a blank button on the panel. It must be another security feature as the button didn't have number near it.

"Mr. Dent will meet you." The doorman smiled and stepped back into the lobby.

"Thank you." Colleen said as the glass door slowly closed and started ascending.

Colleen fussed with her hair in the reflection on the shiny stone wall. When the elevator came to a stop sure enough Brock was standing there waiting for her in the hall. He wore a dark grey button-down shirt tucked into black slacks and a pair of dark dress shoes.

"Hello." He said looking her up and down as she stepped out.

"Hello to you." She smiled and leaned in as he leaned down to kiss.

The week apart had been long and the minute their lips met Colleen felt the fire that had been simmering inside her flare. For a minute she thought they weren't even going to make it into the apartment, let alone make it through dinner.

Brock seemed to sense it too as one of his hands grabbed her waist and the other grazed her thigh.

Slowly he pulled back. "Why don't we go inside, I'd hate to give my neighbors a show."

Colleen laughed slightly breathless. She looped her arm through his and followed him to his unit.

Stepping into Brocks apartment shocked Colleen. Where her apartment was small, bright and light Brocks was warm lighting and dark marble. The entryway opened up into a large living room, the open design leading into the massive kitchen. His walls were dark navy to accent the grey furniture, black marble bar and counters and gold lights. A large window to the right showed a balcony that had a great view of the city. A hallway peeked out just past the kitchen where Colleen assumed the bedrooms were.

"Wow, your place is amazing." Colleen turned and looked at Brock who was looking her up and down.

"No, you look amazing."

Colleen blushed and turned back around, taking in all the details. A large book case sat along the left wall, with a huge assortment of books and small decorative items.

"Care for some wine?" Brock led her past the living room over to the built-in bar. A decanter sat already full of red wine that was breathing.

"Yes, please." She watched as he grabbed the two etched crystal wine goblets and expertly poured wine into them. He passed her one of the glasses. She put her small clutch down on the bar and took a sip. The wine was robust and tasted fantastic. Getting closer to the kitchen she could also start smelling the aromas of dinner.

"Whatcha cooking?" She wandered over, her heels clicking on the dark tile floor.

"I have beef wellington finishing off in the oven, a salad in the fridge and some chocolate covered strawberries for dessert." Brock walked in and cracked open the oven peeking in.

"Well, it smells amazing." She leaned against the counter and watched as he closed the oven and turned back to her.

"I'm excited for you to try it. I hardly ever get the chance to cook for anyone outside of myself."

"And I hardly ever get home cooked meals unless I'm visiting back home. So, it will be nice to eat something not prepared in a commercial kitchen."

Colleen swirled her wine gently and took another sip. The wine was warming her insides.

"So how was your work this week? I feel like we hardly talk about it." She asked shifting her leg to cross her ankles, showing off her legs.

"My works good, I have meetings, make other people money and they are so grateful they keep me around to make more. It's not super exciting." He shrugged and took a drink of his own wine. "It pays well, allows me to live in places like this." He waved his hand around.

"Yeah, this place is definitely something. Can we go look at the balcony?" Colleen asked. She had always imagined having a balcony in New York. Being able to take in the city lights with an evening drink after a long day of work. Or sitting in front of the windows and watching the snow fall in the winter.

"Of course." Brock waved his arm towards the large slider door and walked towards it.

The balcony was everything Colleen had imagined. Brock's building sat out past the neighboring buildings enough to give them an uninterrupted view of the block. The lights from the other apartments and businesses giving the typical city glow everyone thinks of when they imagine New York at night.

Colleen leaned against the rail and took in the view while enjoying her drink. Brock leaned against it next to her. They enjoyed the moment of silence, just listening to the city.

Their silence was interrupted by an alarm chiming on Brock's phone.

"Dinner time." He announced and turned to go back in. Brock left the slider open and walked to the oven. Colleen watched him take the beef wellingtons out and set them on a cooling rack. He grabbed some things out of the fridge and began making two plates of food. He sliced into the main entre and Colleen thought it was adorable when his face lit up in a triumphant smile, the meat obviously cooked exactly to the temperature he was hoping for.

"They look perfect!" He yelled out to her.

"Good, I'm starving." Colleen walked back in just as he brought their plates over to the large dining room table, setting them down next to each other. Colleen set her wine glass next to the pate closest to her and joined Brock for their romantic homecooked dinner.

Chapter Sixteen

Colleen almost licked her plate after the food was gone. She had never had food that good made at home. The meat had been cooked to the perfect temperature and seasoned wonderfully. The small side salad Brock had made that was crisp and flavorful. He had even made the dressing himself.

The finishing touch had been the chocolate covered strawberries. They had been just the right amount of sweetness. When the last berry had been eaten and they had finished off their wine Brock leaned back in his chair.

"Do you want a tour of the rest of the place?" He asked.

"Absolutely." Colleen felt butterflies knowing his end game for their 'tour'.

He stood and reached his hand out for hers. Fingers intertwined they walked down the hallway.

"This is a guest bathroom." He motioned to the open door on the right. Colleen looked in on a dark green powder room with gold accents that matched the main part of the apartment.

"And here is a guest bedroom." He opened a door across from the bathroom. It had a large bed in the center, the room navy and cream colored. A small sitting couch sat on the far wall next to the window.

"Very nice. Did you decorate this place yourself?" Colleen had been curious throughout dinner. Everywhere she looked there was unique touches and designs that all blended well with each other. She thought back to when her parents had redesigned their family home. Her dad could have given two shits what color the sconces were in the living room, let alone if the ones in the bathrooms matched.

"The apartment came with the floor and counters, but I picked the paint and decorated around it. I like art, in all its forms. So, decorating this place I enjoyed." He looked down at her as he led her to the last door in the hall.

"Well, it shows you enjoyed it. I feel like you can always tell in the final result when someone channels their heart into a project." Colleen smiled up at him, loving the joy that was on his face from her compliment.

They reached the final door which was slightly ajar. Slowly he pushed it open to reveal the massive bedroom suite inside.

The room was painted a dark green, also featuring the gold accents from the rest of the house. A king size bed sat against right wall; black satin sheets were revealed where the plush black comforter was expertly turned down. An electric fire place sat on the opposite wall with a decorative armchair in front and a small accent table.

A closed door was near the fireplace, and three tall windows on the far wall had dark brown drapes closed blocking out the lights of the city. Wall sconces were glowing dimly giving the room a warmness to it. Several large pieces of art decorated the walls.

Colleen felt fingers brush the back of her neck, brushing her hair to the side. She felt Brocks lips graze her skin.

"So, what do you think if this room?" He whispered and planted soft kisses down her neck, following her shoulder.

"I think it may be my favorite yet." She whispered back, feeling her breath catch as Brock continued kissing down her collar bone.

She shivered as Brock gently pulled the strap of her dress down, exposing more of her skin.

"Do you want me to turn on the fireplace?" He asked slowly pulling the other strap down. The fabric slid down her body, revealing the lacey bra she wore underneath. She heard Brock grown in approval.

"I think we can find a better way to warm up." Colleen said, slowly working her fingers down the buttons of his shirt.

Brock pushed her dress past her hips, dropping to his knees at the sight of the matching panties.

"You like them?" Colleen asked in a teasing tone. She pushed the open shirt over his shoulders revealing his broad chest.

"Oh, I like them very much." He kissed the inside of her thigh before burying his face between her legs. He grabbed the top of the panties and pulled them slowly down. "Although I think I will like them much better on my floor." She stepped out of them and giggled when he tossed them and they landed in front of the fireplace.

He stood, Colleen catching his face in her hands as he did, bringing his mouth to hers. She nipped his bottom lip as he undid the lace bra, tossing it over his shoulder.

Colleen didn't even care where it landed as she molded her body to his. His hands grabbed her waist and lifted her. She wrapped her legs around his waist as he carried her over to the bed. She could feel him through his pants, rubbing against her as he stepped. She tightened her legs pushing herself against him harder. Brock chuckled.

"Greedy tonight, aren't we?"

Colleen replied by nipping his bottom lip again.

He bent down, lowering her to the bed and shoving the comforter aside. Colleen released her legs, sinking down into the satin sheets, cool against her now fiery skin. She watched as Brock slowly finished undressing. He was hard and ready for her, and Colleen wanted him now.

He crawled across the bed his eyes burning with desire. He took one breast into his mouth licking and sucking until Colleen's back arched up from the bed, her head thrown back. He then released it with a pop and moved to the next.

Colleen knew he was playing with her, and she figured two could play at that game. Slowly she trailed her hands down his back, scraping her nails against his side as her hands went lower, and lower. She grabbed his cock in her hand making him buck against it. She pulled down the length slowly, rubbing her thumb against the tip.

Brock hissed; she could feel the muscles in his back clench under her free hand.

"I want you inside me." Colleen groaned, aching for him.

"Then do it." Brock growled leaning forward.

She moved her hand back up his shaft and guided him to her entrance. She moaned at the feeling of him pressing against her. She released her hand and grabbed his shoulders, signaling to him to take over. He did so greedily, driving deep inside her in one thrust.

"God! You feel good baby." He pulled out slightly before driving back in to the hilt. He set a fast pace that had Colleen arching against his chest. She curled her fingers into his skin, clawing at him.

Colleen moaned, unable to even find words, feeling herself nearing the edge of release already. Brock pulled almost all the way out, and stayed just outside.

"No," Colleen groaned, lifting her head up and staring at him hovering above her. "Don't stop."

Brock shifted, angling himself higher before driving back in, hitting her in that spot on her inner wall.

Colleen felt her eyes roll back and within two more similar moves she screamed out at her release. He pumped into her three more times, until he too found his climax and came apart inside her.

He collapsed on top of her, his head resting beside hers. They laid there, gathering their breath for a moment.

Brock slowly rose up onto his forearms and stared down at Colleen, brushing a stray hair from her face. He was still inside her, and the shift pushed him slightly deeper. Colleen gasped slightly at the movement; her body already ready for another round. Brock's smile grew devilish and he flexed his hips, pushing even more.

"I missed you." He murmured, threading his fingers with hers and pressing them on either side of her head.

"I missed you too." Colleen whispered and smiled wickedly as she wrapped her legs around Brock and pulled their bodies even closer together.

"I don't know how I'm going to stop tonight." He admitted.

"Who's asking you to?" Colleen challenged, her laugh turning into another round of moans as they sank back down into their evening of exploring each other.

Chapter Seventeen

Colleen couldn't believe how much her life had changed in just a few weeks.

It had been a little over a month since the robbery and though she still had lingering nightmares at times Colleen felt like she was moving past the whole situation and readjusting back to her regular life, with her new handsome addition.

There was one incident when a guy had come into the store dressed in all black and a baseball hat that had sent her pulse racing. He had turned out to be a traveling gemstone salesman who had wanted to meet with Roger. Though in any other scenario his attire would have been considered harmless, Colleen had to call Brock from the backroom to be calmed down.

She also felt better when she heard Roger chastise the salesman for his choice of attire since he knew about the string of robberies.

Three more stores had been hit in the month. They had estimated that the amount of stolen merchandise had crested the million-dollar mark. The news noting the increase time between hits increasing. One theory was he was running out of places to hit, another that the police had caught a lead and he was trying to be more careful. But no one could say for sure.

Though the mystery of the robberies was still hanging around, Colleen found her relationship with Brock growing stronger. Last week he had even joined one of her evening facetime's with her parents, introducing himself as her boyfriend and answered all of her mother's intrusive and random questions.

Colleen had gotten a long text the next morning from her mom expressing her approval in Brock. Which she had read to him while they ordered their coffee from Carlos before work.

"Well, that's good she likes you." Colleen laughed while grabbing her to go cup from Carlos. "Even four states away she could make life very difficult if she hadn't."

"Then I am also very glad she likes me." Brock picked his cup off the counter where he had secured his lid down.

They had walked out together and Brock flagged a cab down to take him to his fist client meeting of the day. As the yellow cab detoured from the flow of traffic he turned to Colleen.

"By the way, I wanted to ask you if you wanted to go away with me this weekend?"

"Go away where?" Colleen asked as the cab slowed up to the curb. Butterflies fluttered in her stomach. She had never been in a relationship long enough, or serious enough to ever 'go away' with.

"I have a small house upstate I bought shortly after moving here. It's been a bit since I've been up there and wanted to see if you wanted to join me?" He opened the door to the cab but waited a moment to get in until she answered.

"Sure, that sounds like it would be a lot fun." She clutched her coffee in both hands and smiled up at him.

His face broke into a large grin and he ducked down to give her a quick kiss before getting in the cab.

"I'll talk to you later and send you all the details." He said as he closed the door. Colleen waved as the cab pulled away.

True to his word Brock had been texting her most of the morning about his "small upstate house" that turned out to be more of a cabin.

They had agreed to head up after work Friday. And Colleen had spent the whole week fussing. She wasn't sure what to pack for their weekend. She had never been upstate in her time in New York and with the spring weather she wasn't sure if she should bring shorts and dresses, or flannels and jeans. She felt silly asking Brock so come Friday she had ended up with two bags for their weekend. One full of long sleeves, jeans and a jacket. The other with shorts and blouses. Both though contained more of the little lacey 'art' Brock loved.

Colleen had gotten one of her neighbors who she was friendly with to agree to check in on Mochi. And Brock had rented a car, parking it in a temp spot in front of the building to help Colleen bring her bags down. He loaded them into the trunk, stacking them on top of his own packed bags of clothes and some bags of groceries he had stopped and picked up on the way. If he thought her two bags were ridiculous, he didn't say. He just smiled like a kid getting ready to go to Disney Land as they made their way through the typical New York traffic to head out of the city. Colleen felt a sense of relief when the roads slowly cleared as they made their way further from the chronic city congestion.

When they drove farther the scenes outside the window slowly changed from tall skyscrapers and taxi cabs to some industrial buildings and suburban neighborhoods.

As they kept driving the houses began spreading out further apart. More trees became noticeable, and it was more obvious they were growing there naturally and had not been transplanted for looks by whoever built the homes.

They passed the drive listening to each other's favorite podcasts. Brock had broken out a bag of snacks and Colleen had opened up the gummy bears and popcorn for them to share.

Colleen also noticed Brock relaxing the further out of the city they got. She had wondered how stressful his job was. Though he didn't like to talk about it much Colleen had heard about how the corporate finance positions could affect people. She was glad he was getting a break, and that he had invited her to come along.

"It's just about ten miles or so up the road." Brock announced as they pulled off the main highway. Forests had slowly integrated into the landscape, separating out the houses further and further.

Their speed lowered and Colleen used the opportunity to roll her window down and feel the cool air on her face. She inhaled deeply, loving the fresh pine scent that filled her lungs. It reminded her of the woods back home. The trees were the thing she missed in the city. Real trees, not the carefully trimmed and upkept "pretty" ones the city chose to grow in designated park areas. A smile grew on her face and when she looked over at Brock, he was sneaking glances at her between curves on the road. His smile at hers sent her heart racing and she couldn't wait for their weekend alone.

Chapter Eighteen

The house Brock owned was tucked away down a small dirt driveway, hidden away into the forest around it. Colleen had expected a rustic cabin similar to the neighbors but instead was met with a very modern concept. She could tell the dark brown siding was new, as well as the black metal roof and matching trim. Solar panels were cleanly lined up on top of the high points in the roof allowing some to grab the morning light, and the others the evening.

The yard was landscaped with a circling driveway that allowed them to pull up beside the house. Brock came around and opened the door for Colleen. As soon as she stepped out, he popped the trunk and began grabbing bags. He had hers and some of the groceries in his arms as he walked up the large wooden steps to the porch.

"Come on in." He gestured his head towards the door. Colleen followed.

The inside of the house was as modern as his apartment, though he had kept some woodland charm. Instead of cool blacks and navys he had kept with some warmer browns and matching creams. It was very open, the large living room had tall back windows that viewed out to the forest behind the property, a large brick fireplace was built as the divider of the space. A kitchen was just behind it, clearly by the large stainless-steel appliances he did not skip the luxuries of the modern world while out here 'roughing it'. A cozy looking couch sat in front of the fireplace while still positioned to enjoy the views out the windows. A hallway led towards the bedrooms. The smaller ones Colleen guessed were Guest rooms had cute rustic furniture and plaid bedding.

The main bedroom was decorated in dark woodland greens with matching rich brown furniture. A large split his and hers walkthrough closet led to the bathroom that had a massive soaking clawfoot tub sitting beside another set of large arching windows that viewed more of the dense forest.

"Don't worry." Brock whispered in her ear when she had paused to admire the tub. "I own enough of the property around here we don't have to worry about any stray neighbors spotting us in the tub later." Colleen felt her toes curl in her shoes at the idea of both of them in the tub.

"Well, that's good." She whispered back.

He chuckled and kissed her neck before heading back to the car and getting more of the bags.

Colleen followed to help.

"I think one fell in the middle row there, can you grab it?" Brock asked as he walked past her into the house with a duffle bag and the last few groceries.

"Sure." Colleen moved to the back passenger door and opened it. She spied the green plastic bag that had tumbled from the seat. She leaned down and grabbed at the handles and pulled, trying the keep anything from spilling. The bag snagged on something; Colleen crawled in further to see what the obstruction was.

It appeared a black bag was tucked under the seat as well, the plastic grocery bag catching in the bags zipper. She grabbed the black material and pulled. A black backpack emerged and for a second Colleen was shocked at a memory that flooded back to her. A memory of a black backpack that had looked identical to this one, in her shaking hands as a knife was pushed into her neck. Quickly Colleen shoved the backpack away from her back under the seat. Her hands shaking slightly and sweaty from the memory. She shook herself; she was being ridiculous. It was just a backpack. Every man in New York probably had similar looking bags, so it wasn't odd that Brock had one too. Maybe it was his work bag and he didn't want her to know he had snuck work with him and that's why he left it in the car. But that eerie feeling refused to go away, no matter how many times she tried to shake it.

Colleen carefully worked the grocery bag out of the zipper and shoved the backpack back under the seat where she had found it and closed the car door. Brock was coming out of the bedroom as she entered the house. He smiled at her as he walked to the kitchen and began putting food away in the cupboards and fridge. She followed, eyeing him as he moved about.

She wasn't sure why the backpack was giving her such an uneasy feeling. She was just about to ask him if he wanted her to bring the backpack that was under the seat in when she stopped herself.

Was she really going to do that? Accuse the man she had been seeing, the best man she had ever dated and the one who planned this amazing getaway of what? Being the criminal who held her at knife point? And all over a backpack that he may not have been trying to hide in the first place. Perhaps it had also gotten shaken from the journey and he just hadn't noticed it was missing yet.

"Is everything okay?" Brock asked breaking her internal argument. She realized she had just been standing there, her hands had curled into the plastic handles of the grocery back, straining the plastic and turning her fingers bright red.

"Yeah, I'm fine. Sorry I just got caught up in a thought." She untwined her fingers from the bag and set it on the counter. Brock moved around the large island and gathered her in his arms.

She leaned into him, allowing his scent to wash away all her dark thoughts. There was no way this man would do anything to hurt someone.

"What do you say I go get that bath started?" He whispered into her hair, his hands rubbing up and down her back.

"Sure, that sounds nice. I can finish putting this stuff away." She looked up into his eyes and saw they held a tint of concern. He seemed to be able to sense she was still worrying over something. "I'm okay, I promise." She got up on her tip toes and kissed him.

"Okay." He said between kissing her back.

"One bath coming up." He gave her a playful slap on the ass which got her squealing and running around the island. He chuckled as he walked around the corner to the bathroom.

Colleen started putting more of the food away. There were a few insulated bags left with cold items she made to put in the fridge.

She couldn't fight the smile at the can of whip cream she pulled out. From the looks of what else was in there she didn't think Brock planned to put this on ice cream.

The sound of water filling the tub echoed through the house. Colleen rushed to put the rest of the food into any spot it would fit in the pantry. As the last cupboard closed, she heard the water faucet get turned off. She kicked her shoes off, letting them thump on the ground and slowly undressed herself as she made her way to the bathroom.

Chapter Nineteen

Brock had dimmed the lights in the bathroom, letting it be mostly lit from the tall picture window. The scent of roses filled the air as Colleen walked in, now completely unclothed, her hair pulled up into a bun.

She found Brock already lounging in the tub, bubbles rounded up almost to the edge. He reached a hand out and held her steady as she stepped in to join him. The water was warm, and relaxed her instantly.

Brock arranged her to lay between his legs, she leaned back and rested against his chest, his arms wrapped around her.

Colleen couldn't help the large sigh she let out as the water relaxed her muscles, her head leaning against his shoulder.

"I've dreamed of this moment." Brock said, his voice rough.

"Oh yeah?" She tilted her head up to glance at him.

"As soon as I saw this room, I dreamed of having someone I wanted to bring here and do just this." He squeezed her a little.

"Just this?" Colleen asked in a teasing tone.

"This, and this." He leaned down and kissed her neck below her ear. "And this." He traced his mouth around her jaw, his hands also shifting under the water, lightly trailing up and down her sides.

"And this." He captured her mouth in his. His hands gathered both her breasts and squeezed. Colleen moaned, the sound triggering his body. She could feel him harden against her back.

He trailed his mouth back down to her neck, his hands roamed down her stomach, between her legs. His fingers danced around, teasing her.

Colleen arched into his touch, wanting more. His left hand splayed across her stomach, holding her in place while his right hand continued its teasing. He slowly played with her, swirling his finger around her clit before sliding it inside her, teasing her. She could feel her climax slowly building inside her. But just before she could find her release Brock withdrew his fingers. She tried to protest, but he grabbed both of her legs and pulled them apart, lifting her up and angling her right above him.

Slowly he lowered her down on top of his cock.

Colleen bit her lip in pleasure to keep from calling out as he filled her slowly. She gripped the edge of the tub with both hands, trying to hold herself in place as he slowly lifted his hips to meet her.

Brock had filled the tub expertly, no water splashed out as he slowly bucked his hips up in an easy rhythm. Colleen had already been close so it only took a few thrusts before she screamed out in release. Her head threw back against Brock's shoulder, she could feel his muscles clench behind her as he also finished.

They laid there in the water for several moments until their breathing returned to normal. Brock had skillfully separated their bodies and returned them to their earlier lounging position.

Colleen looked out the window at the trees, she noticed a stone fire pit with a set of wooden lounge style chairs and matching wine barrel table.

"Ooo, are we going to have a fire?" Colleen asked looking up at Brocks content face.

"We can do anything you want." He said, still a little breathless, making her laugh.

"Well, I hope you brought marshmallows then, because I make one mean s'more."

This caused Brock to join her laughter.

"Oh I brought all the fixings for smores."

"Good." Colleen settled her head back and closed her eyes, enjoying the moment and looking forward to their weekend.

Chapter Twenty

As soon as the water started to cool Brock got out and grabbed one of the fluffy grey towels from the built-in shelf and tied it around his waist. Colleen enjoyed the view from the tub, waiting for him to finish and grab a towel for her.

"Were you staring at my ass?" He asked in a false accusatory tone as he turned around holding another towel.

"Why yes, yes, I was. And a fine ass it is." Colleen said very formally, standing as she did. She stepped out of the water, dripping bubbles onto the soft bath mat below her feet. She held her arms out to the sides causing Brock to laugh as he walked forward and wrapped the towel around her.

He leaned his head down and kissed her, his hands slowly tucking the end of the towel into the front of the wrap.

Just then a cell phone started ringing from the bedroom.

"Did you keep your phone on?" Colleen asked, slowly pulling back.

Brock let out a deep sigh.

"I did, but I told them to only call if it was an emergency. So, I should probably go see what it is they are wanting."

"Fine, I guess I will go get dressed then." Colleen followed him into the closet, staying back to go through her bags that were set on one side while Brock walked through to the bedroom.

The ringing stopped and she could hear Brock's voice say a rough greeting to whoever was on the other end.

Colleen fished out a pair of black leggings, a cream tank top and a red flannel she may or may not have bought specifically for this trip. She then pulled on a pair of thick comfy socks and a pair of Chelsea boots.

She could still hear Brock muttering sternly on the phone as she pulled her hair from the elastic holding it up and finger combed the underside to keep any of the damp pieces from tangling.

"That is not how we do things, and you know it!" Brock suddenly shouted, startling Colleen. She had never heard him angry before.

She slowly poked her head out into the bedroom and looked for him. He was standing in front of the tall windows, looking out. The grey towel still draped around his hips. The muscles of his back were tensed as he held his phone up to his ear.

"No, I will not be a part of that deal." He stated. There was a pause as the other person said something back to him. "Yes well, I don't care how much money it is. I don't work that way. So best of luck to ya."

At that he clicked to hang up the call. Brock stood there; the phone gripped so tightly in his hand Colleen worried he would crack the screen.

"Everything okay?" She asked quietly, slowly walking out of the closet into the bedroom.

He turned, his jaw tight and the skin on his throat was flushed from anger. Colleen had seen Brock in many moods in their time together, but she had never seen him truly angry before.

"Yes, it's fine. One of the guys I work with isn't handling a deal the way we are supposed to. It's going to end up blowing up in his face, but he doesn't seem to care. He wanted to see if I would back him, make the deal look more legit. But that's not how I do things." He relaxed his hand on his phone, tossing it lightly onto the bed and rubbing his face with both hands.

"So, if what he's doing is wrong, are you going to out him to your bosses?" Colleen crossed her arms and leaned against the arm of one of the sitting chairs.

"I won't have to. The way he's trying, it doesn't work. The deal will blow up in his face, and that will be that." He rubbed a hand against the back of his head. "It's just frustrating. But I don't want to keep thinking about it. In fact." He moved towards the bed and picked the phone back up. He pressed against the side button, holding it down until the phone shut itself off completely.

"There, now no more interruptions." He looked up and smiled at her. Colleen smiled back, though she could tell the phone call was still bothering him.

"Why don't you go grab some of the wood from the shed and bring it over to the fire pit while I get dressed? We can have some wine and enjoy the sunset by the fire?" He leaned forward and grabbed the edges of her flannel, tugging her forward against him.

"Or... you can just stay in your little towel." Colleen teased, walking two of her fingers along his bare chest. She succeeded in getting Brock to chuckle.

"If it wasn't for the bugs, I'd probably take you up on that. But since nothing is as unsexy as mosquito bites, I think I will opt for some clothes."

Colleen mocked a disappointed face and sighed out an exaggerated "Fiinne". Brock released her and made his way to the closet.

"And don't even think about trying to look at my ass again." He shot over his shoulder.

"Your no fun!" Colleen yelled back "But I demand tomorrow you re-enact some very interesting videos I've seen online of handsome muscular men chopping wood shirtless!"

"Deal!" She heard yelled back to her before making her way out to the backyard.

Chapter Twenty-One

Colleen found the small wood shed off to the side of the house beside the wall to the bedroom. It was packed full of split logs, and she had to fight off the vision of watching Brock chop wood shirtless in the woods.

There was a pair of thick leather gloves sitting on a small worktable next to an ax and what looked like a thicker, bulkier ax. After inspecting the fingers and making sure no eight legged creepy crawlies were present, she slipped on the too large gloves and grabbed a chunk of wood in each hand.

Colleen worked for a few minutes, taking logs two at a time from the shed and moving them to a small pile by the chairs. She took a small break, leaning against one of the chairs and used the back of her hand to brush some stray hair back from her face. From here she could see through the windows into the bedroom and the living room.

Colleen caught a flash of movement and light from the living room. She leaned slightly to better see and Brock was coming back in from the front door. He didn't seem to notice her as he turned and closed the door, a black backpack thrown over one shoulder.

A sense of unease settled into Colleen's gut like a stone. She stood and made her way casually back across the lawn, acting as if she was just making another trip for wood. She glanced back through the windows and saw Brock stride quickly through the living room, making his way to the bedroom.

Colleen moved, tucking herself close to the shed that was just out of site from the bedroom windows. She used her position to peek in around the corner. Hoping the evening twilight would help hide her.

Brock came in the bedroom, shooting a glance out the windows. His eyes scanned the fire pit area, Colleen ducked quickly. Hoping if he saw her, he would think she was just grabbing more wood.

After a second, she popped her head back around and Brock had disappeared into the closet, the bag with him. She angled her head, hoping to catch sight of which side of the closet he had gone too but she couldn't see past the doorway.

Slowly she made her way back to the firepit and sat on one of the chairs, the wood cool from the shade that had grown across the yard with the sun dipping behind the trees. Colleen stared blankly at the empty firepit, trying to decipher why the site of the bag was bothering her so much. He hadn't been rifling through it like she would have expected if it had contained clothing or toiletries he had been searching for. Something about that backpack was off and she knew she was going to have to figure out what was inside it.

The sound of the backdoor opening and closing drew her from her thoughts. Brock grinned as he walked across the yard holding a tray with a large assortment of food, a blanket also draped over his arm.

He sat the tray down and Colleen could see it held hotdogs, buns, and all the ingredients for s'mores.

"I think we should do a full fire pit cook out tonight." Brock said draping the blanket he held over the back of the chair Colleen was sitting at. "I'll go grab the roasting sticks." He went up to the shed where the firewood was stored and came back with two metal sticks with wooden handles.

"How rustic." Colleen laughed. The man who had insisted on cooking top tier meals for them when she didn't feel like going out was now so excited for a method of cooking, she hadn't done since she was a child.

"Right? I thought it would be fun." He handed one of the poles to her and leaned his own against the table. Grabbing some of the small kindling pieces Colleen had piled next to the larger wood stack he began building the structure for their fire.

Within moments he had it lit thanks to a small lighter also on the tray. He began gradually adding larger pieces of wood to the stack until they had a blazing fire. Just in time for the sun to sink further, sending the yard into darkness aside from the glow from the fire and the few lights that had been left on in the house.

Brock threaded a hotdog onto each of their poles and while Colleen successfully charred the outside of hers, Brock showed he was just as exceptional cooking over a fire as he was a stove. He'd offered to cook her a new one, but Colleen secretly liked the slightly charcoal flavor of burnt hotdogs and had insisted on eating hers just as she'd cooked it.

Colleen relaxed as they chatted and laughed over the fire, slowly forgetting again her worries over the mysterious backpack. She was grateful for the blanket, even though the fire was warming her front, she draped it over her shoulders to help keep the cool evening air from rushing down her back.

Their s'mores cooking closely resembled their hotdogs. Brocks was a lightly toasted gold, perfect for melting the chocolate. Colleens had dipped to far into the fire and had come up engulfed in flames. They had laughed as Brock leaned forward quickly and blew it out. He then had handed her his and went about making another one.

Colleen had forgotten how much she loved s'mores. The gooey mix of marshmallow and melted chocolate was the perfect combination. She settled back into her blanket and enjoyed her treat while watching Brock lean back into his chair with his again perfectly cooked marshmallow.

"I love it out here." He sighed taking a bite into his desert, causing marshmallow to squeeze out the side and almost smash into his face.

Colleen chuckled and handed him a napkin from the tray.

"It's so quiet and peaceful. I can see why you like it out here." She glanced up at the night sky, marveling at how many stars she could see. "I can't even remember the last time I saw a star that wasn't on a digital billboard."

"I know, that's the bummer of the city. No stars and its never quiet." Brock also tilted his head up and admired the night time view.

Colleen pulled her blanket around her shoulders, nestling in and enjoying the coziness of the evening. She hadn't even realized she had begun drifting off until a pair of strong arms gently lifted her from the chair and cradled her against an equally strong chest.

She leaned her head onto Brock's shoulder as he carried her back up to the house. She was asleep again before they reached the door.

Chapter Twenty-Two

When Colleen woke the next morning, she thought for a second, she was still by the fire pit. It took her a second the realize the faint smell of smoke wasn't coming from an active flame, but was coming from her hair that apparently was clinging onto the scent.

Brock had taken her out of her clothes and shoes she had been wearing, putting her in one of the sleep shirts she had packed. But the smell of smoke still clung to her hair, burning her nose slightly.

She rolled over to see the bed empty beside her. The sun had already begun to rise, the sky a pale blue out the window.

Colleen got out of bed and padded to the kitchen. Brock was nowhere to be seen, but a small piece of paper was folded and propped up for her attention on the counter.

Good morning love,

I went for a run and will be gone for a bit. The coffee pot is filled, just press the Brew button. I'll be back in a bit.

Love

Brock

Colleen smiled at the note. One of the first weeks of their relationship he had tried to convince her to go on one of his ridiculous morning runs. She had laughed as she rolled back over and pulled the covers over her head. Colleen's physique was thanks to good genes and her commuting by foot everywhere. Outside of that she had on occasion been convinced by a girlfriend to attend the random yoga class. But she was no runner. So that was something Brock got to do alone, and was apparently something he still did even on vacation.

She wandered over to the coffee machine that looked way more professional than anything she could figure out. So, she was glad he had already preprogrammed everything for her. A small button glowed lightly that had the word 'Brew' printed on it.

Colleen pressed the button and the machine slowly revved its little motor and began dispensing coffee and creamer into the cup Brock had also placed under it.

When it signaled it was finished with a little sing-song chime Colleen grabbed the heated cup with two hands and went to sit in one of the arm chairs next to the indoor fireplace that looked out into the woods.

She enjoyed the peace of the morning, sipping her coffee until it was all gone. It was delicious, and if she had any idea on how the machine worked, she would have made herself another cup. But with all of the buttons and compartments she chose instead to rinse out the cup and go wash the smell of smoke out of her hair.

The large walk-in shower had a waterfall style shower head coming out of the ceiling that Colleen was going to suggest to Brock he get installed in the shower at his apartment as well if he could. She shampooed twice to get all the ashy smell out, replacing it with a citrus scent that's bottles she was also going to ask Brock to stock at home.

Deciding Brock would probably enjoy some hot water too when he came back from his run Colleen begrudgingly got out of the shower, wrapping one of the large towels around her. She was just about to walk through to the side of the closet where her bags sat when she caught site of something from the other side, where Brocks clothes were stored. She walked around the wall that split the sides and spied the black backpack propped against a built-in drawer system, half unzipped.

Colleen paused and listened; the house still silent, and there wasn't the sound of crunching rocks under tennis shoes coming from outside. She leaned down and grabbed the bag, unzipping it the rest of the way. Inside looked the same as any backpack, just one main open compartment inside. And inside was, completely empty.

Colleen frowned. She hadn't picked the bag up when she found it in the car, but from its shape she was sure something had been inside it. Holding the empty bag in her hand she glanced around. The closet looked like it had before. Brock kept a permanent 'rustic' wardrobe here. Flannel shirts hung up on the racks, boots and a pair of slippers sat on the built-in shoe rack. Colleen glanced down at the drawers and noticed one was slightly open still, having caught possibly on the backpack that had been sitting on the floor against it, preventing it from closing all the way.

Putting the bag back where she had found it Colleen slowly pulled the drawer open. Inside the drawer though was just perfectly organized rolled up socks. The most practical reason being he had grabbed socks for his run this morning and in his hurry to get out of the closet without waking Colleen in the bedroom he hadn't gotten the drawer closed all the way.

But the uneasy feeling in Colleen's gut would not go away. She carefully moved some of the socks aside, looking to see if anything was hidden under them. Nothing but the dark wood of the drawer bottom was there. Sighing she went to place back the handful of socks in her hand. But when the knuckle of one of her fingers tapped the bottom of the drawer the hallow echo gave her pause.

She set the socks on the ground and ran her fingers along the edges of the drawer, sliding the remaining socks around as she did, until her fingers grazed a small half circle hole near the back.

Colleen held her breath as she slowly lifted the false bottom of the drawer revealing small black boxes tucked perfectly together in a single layer. She dropped the piece of wood, nearly missing her still bare toes. Her hands shook as she reached down and grabbed a long slim box.

The exterior was velvety and soft against her still damp skin as she opened the lid.

A choked sound came out of Colleen as she revealed a very familiar diamond and sapphire bracelet pinned carefully inside the box.

It was the same bracelet she had worked so hard to display that morning weeks ago. The same rare shade of blue, the same sparkling bright diamonds. The same bracelet she had been forced to dump into a basic black backpack with a knife held to her throat.

Colleen's vision blurred, and she wasn't sure if it was from the tears building, or from the uncontrollable shaking her whole body was doing. She honestly wasn't sure if she was about to pass out or not. Either way she slowly sank to her knees, the towel pooling on the ground around her as she stared at the bracelet.

She didn't need to open the other boxes to figure out what was inside them, she knew she would find the rest of the matching sapphire suite.

Then the memory of all the other robberies rang through her head and she glanced up at the dozen built in drawers that sat in front of her.

Did they all have false bottoms? How many stolen pieces were stashed away here? She glanced around the full closet wondering how many other hidey holes were here. Did he hoard everything like a dragon? Or was this just the holding location for him to sell the pieces as buyers became available.

Her memory flashed to the phone call he took last night. Did he even have a job in the finance district? Or had that been a lie too. Was the coworker someone else who was in on this whole thing? Colleen's eyes kept scanning the rows of drawers around her when she noticed the empty spot on the shoe rack where Brock kept his running shoes. It suddenly reminded her she was on very limited time schedule.

She wasn't sure when he had left for his run, or how far he was going. Colleen shot to her feet; she was still naked from her shower. Clutching the bracelet box in her hand she knew she had a decision to make.

Did she put everything back and pretend she never saw it? Or did she flee? She had always prided herself on that she was a good person. She had never done anything outwardly "bad" in her life. She had even felt bad when she had kept a library book past its return by date. And now here she was dating one of New York's most prolific diamond thieves. And she knew deep down she should turn him in. But the ache in her heart was keeping her from reaching for her phone that was sitting in her bag and calling the police.

She had known the feelings were there for a while now, and her new discovery should have immediately changed them... but it didn't.

Colleen Scott was in love with New York's most prolific diamond thief.

And it was with that knowledge plaguing her heart that she threw the bracelet in her bag and got dressed as fast as she could.

She had her phone in hand, bags over her shoulder and was grabbing the car keys Brock had hung by the door in under five minutes. She had left the closet a mess, not bothering to put the false bottom or socks back in the drawer. She wanted him to know that she knew his secret. That was also why she had taken the bracelet with her. She wasn't sure how this was going to play out yet. But she wanted proof, she wanted evidence to hold onto until she figure it all out.

Her bags were thrown in the back of the car and she was speeding back down the forest road, still no sign of Brock. Dirt and rock flung out around her as she drove as fast as she could. If he was running on the road, she wanted to make sure she had passed him before he even recognized the car and tried to stop her.

She didn't let a muscle relax until she hit the highway and was driving back to the city. But it was almost like a trigger. The moment the tires hit the pavement of the highway her cellphone rang loudly, Brock's name lighting up her screen. She glanced from the road and watched it ring.

She did the same thing the three more times it rang.

Chapter Twenty-Three

Colleen used the long drive back to the city to try to piece together some kind of plan.

She was in love with not only a thief, she was in love with the thief that had held a knife to her throat and demanded she dump tens of thousands of dollars' worth of jewelry into a bag before zip tying her wrists and leaving her on the floor of Campbells before fleeing with the afore mentioned jewelry. Jewelry it appeared he had been holding onto along with thousands of dollars more from other stores he robbed. Jewelry he then stowed it away with them on the way to their romantic getaway under the backseat essentially making her a victim and an accomplice.

Had it always been a part of his plan to get involved with her? She felt a knot twist in her gut at the thought that he had only gotten close to her to get close to the store. Was he going to use her to rob them again?

He had always asked her about the store, but she had thought he was just being thoughtful and showing interest in what she did. Colleen now thought back to how vague he had always been about his own job when she had tried to reciprocate the interest.

Her cellphone rang again. This was the fourth time he had tried to call her. This time she clicked the side button, sending him to voicemail.

She needed space and time. Both she effectively would get since she stole the rental car and left him abandoned at his stash house hours away from the city. She wasn't sure what to do with the car once she got back home. Brock had picked it up before picking her up, but she figured that was his problem.

Then a thought popped into her head that started an outburst of hysterical giggles.

Why would he care about getting in trouble for not returning a rental car in time? He had robbed at least twelve jewelry stores over the past year. The news had reported his total amount stolen was estimated in the millions. And that was just from the stores he robbed outwardly in the day. She had no idea what he did the nights he wasn't with her. Or what he had done before he had come to New York.

As she pulled into the busy city traffic on the bridge, she made a mental note to look up if any high-profile robberies had happened along the west coast. He had made a mention once over dinner how the food at the restaurant they were at reminded him of a place he like in San Francisco, so she would start there.

Traffic was busy for a Sunday morning, the cabs were out in full force, honking while cutting in and out of lanes. Colleen felt her palms start to sweat as she clenched her hands around the steering wheel. There was a reason she had given up driving when she moved to the city like so many others. The traffic here was brutal, and the drivers even worse. Not a single car on the road was damage free. Even the rental she drove now she had noticed had some dents on the bumper.

The last thing she needed today was a car accident. So, she took her time and slowly made her way to her apartment.

The street was packed, so Colleen pulled the car down the block a way. She grabbed all of her bags in one go and carried them down the street and up the stairs.

When she unlocked her apartment Mochi greeted her with a happy little meow. Colleen sighed as she dumped her bags on the ground and rolled out her shoulders. Why had she packed so much stuff? She chastised herself. She ran across the hall to let her neighbor know she was home early and didn't need her to check in on Mochi anymore.

When she walked back through her front door, she paused and took the keys to the car and dropped them just past the little welcome mat she had, knowing he would find them whenever he was able to get a ride back here and would ultimately show up at her door.

She knew her apartment would be the first place he stopped. So, she went to work. There was one thing she was sure about; that time he had gotten in claiming she had simply left the door unlocked she hadn't been crazy. He had simply picked the lock and came in.

One of the best parts about living in the city, she was able to get on her phone and order everything she needed to secure her place and have it delivered right to her door within the hour without ever needing to leave her apartment.

In the mean time she had pushed a decorative cabinet she had kept just off to the left of the door in front of the door. Giving her a sense of security so that she could go and unpack her bags.

Unzipping her duffle, she saw the long black box nestled on top and paused. She wasn't sure what to do with it now, and she was feeling uneasy about taking possession of it. Especially since it was a piece from her own robbery.

But she couldn't go back in time and not take it, so she grabbed the box and wandered around her apartment trying to find a place to hide it that wouldn't be so obvious. She settled on dumping out the box of breadcrumbs that were outdated. He had already made a comment once when he had tried to cook a meal in her kitchen on the date and had opened the box to look at the breadcrumbs inside to see if they were still good. She had grouched about them still being good and he had put the box back in the cupboard, so he wouldn't question the box being open. She carefully placed the bracelet in the emptied box, refolded the top and put it back into the cupboard.

With that simple task done Colleen could feel the adrenaline she had been running off of all morning slowly start to dwindle. It allowed her to start trying to formulate a long-term plan outside of "flee the scene."

"What the fuck am I going to do now?" She muttered, hoping the universe would give her some kind of answer.

Chapter Twenty-Four

The knock on Colleen's door sent her jumping nearly through her roof. She put her hand on her chest, to still her heartbeat when she remembered her delivery. Her phone chimed with a text of a picture of the bag sitting by her front door.

Still shaking slightly, Colleen pushed her cabinet out of the way and peeked out her door before grabbing the bag and ducking back inside.

She didn't bother trying to get a new lock, she had never given Brock a key and she knew if he could pick one lock, he could pick another.

Instead, she had placed the order with a small store she knew of just around the corner that sold home defense devices. She pulled out a tension pole that was meant to lean just under your door knob, effectively keeping someone from opening your door when it was in place. She also pulled out of the bag an item that looked like a door stop. But what it had on top was a pressure plate that when pushed down emitted a loud siren that would wake up her and probably her whole floor when it sounded. This she would use as her last step of defense in case he was able to get past the deadbolt and the pole, at least this way he couldn't surprise her in the shower or when she was asleep.

Of course, these devices only helped when she was home. Colleen wasn't sure yet what she was going to do to keep him from getting in when she was at work.

She could move, but she liked her apartment. The rent was stable and easy to afford with her pay. And it was the perfect location to everything she needed.

She had already asked off through Monday with the intention of spending it in a romantic woodland retreat. Instead, though she would use the time to figure out what she was going to do.

Colleen spent the rest of the day on edge. Feeling like a prisoner in her home she was restless, moving from one room to another. She had turned the TV on for a little bit but every channel seemed to take a break from whatever show it was playing to provide updates and ask for tips in regards to the jewel thief terrorizing New York's diamond district. Finally, she had to turn it off and chose to spend the day in silence, internally struggling with what she should do.

She knew she should go to the police. She should hand in the bracelet and report everything she had found. But then a memory of Brock's smile, or the way he would gently swipe the hair from her face when they were lying in bed would flash into her mind. Could that really be the same man who had held a knife to her throat? But how else could he have gotten the jewelry? The mental debate continued until Colleen thought her brain would melt.

Her phone had also stayed noticeably silent. It lay on her counter, blank except for the notification reminders of the calls he had made earlier. She suspected he was driving, or had gotten a ride. Either way too busy getting back to the city to try to contact her again. Plus, he had probably gotten the point that she was not going to answer him.

Colleen had just finished making a cup of instant soup and was settling on the couch to watch Mochi play with her toy mouse when the knock she had dreaded echoed through her apartment.

It was heavy and deliberate, echoing through the apartment. Even Mochi seemed to sense to tension and fled into the bedroom to hide.

Colleen slowly set the cup down on the side table and stood, though she didn't take a step towards the door. Her heart was pounding in her chest.

The knock echoed again.

"Colleen." Brock's voice followed. When she didn't answer he called her again.

"Colleen, I know you're in there, can we please talk?" His voice didn't sound angry or even annoyed. If anything, there was a touch of sadness to it that for a moment made Colleen want to open the door.

But she fought that feeling as she slowly walked towards the door.

"I don't want to talk to you." She said loud enough for him to hear, but not loud enough to draw the attention of the neighbors.

"I need you to leave, and don't come back here or I'll call the police."

She could hear him pick up the keys she had dropped out front for him and then silence. He hadn't tried to come in.

Colleen stood there for a few more minutes, her heart slowing down and her mind reeling about his reaction. Or lack thereof.

She sat back down in her chair and picked her soup back up. She took a few bites, the broth and noodles now cold. Her eyes never leaving the door, her eyes searching for any signs of the door handle moving.

But it never did.

Eventually the apartment grew dark as the sky did. Colleen wandered over to the window and looked up at the night sky. Black but seemingly still lit up thanks to the city lights, not a star to be seen.

How had it been only twenty-four hours ago they were just a normal couple stargazing?

Colleen felt empty inside, hallow. So many feelings had pumped through her this weekend, and they all had seemed to drain out of her, leaving her an emotionless shell.

Climbing into her bed she thought about how she hadn't cried yet. The man she loved had betrayed her, had based their entire relationship off of his crime against her. Had used her vulnerability afterwards to gain favor and worm his way into her life and her heart. And she still hadn't shed a single tear.

Mochi jumped onto the bed and curled up in her usual place by Colleens legs. She purred quietly; happy Colleen was home and wanting to snuggle. At least for now, Colleen was sure she'd be back to her normal sassy self tomorrow morning.

But Colleen closed her eyes and focused on the cats' soft purrs, allowing them to drift her into sleep. And escape the terrible day she'd had.

Chapter Twenty-Five

Colleen's breath hitched in her throat as his lips pulled from hers and traveled down her body.

She arched into him as his hot breath seemed to scorch her skin.

"Brock!" She gasped, aching for him to stop playing with her. He had been teasing her for what felt like hours. Taking her to the edge and stopping just before her release.

"Shh…" He whispered, his hands grabbing hers and pinning them over her head against the pillows.

"I have something special for you." He teased into her ear.

"What?" She groaned, lifting her hips and pressing them against his.

He chuckled deeply; she could tell he wanted her. But he was having too much fun playing.

He released one of her hands, and she felt something cold against her still captured wrist. When he let it go, he sat back, looking expectantly at her.

"Do you like it?" He asked and she pulled her arm down and looked at her wrist.

A familiar sapphire and diamond bracelet was locked onto her wrist, flashing in the city lights that came in through the window. Colleen looked at it in horror, she glanced back at Brock. He still sat in front of her on the bed, but now he was wearing the same dark outfit with the neck of his sweater pulled up half his face as he had the day he had robbed Campbells. An unfolded pocket knife glinted in his hand.

Colleen screamed and shot up in bed, waking herself from her nightmare.

She was alone, no one sat on her bed. She looked down at her bare wrists, her skin had a sheen from sweat.

"It was just a dream." She assured herself while untangling her legs from the sheets.

She padded to the kitchen and grabbed a glass from the cupboard and filled it from the faucet. She took a big gulp, letting the chilled water cool her down.

Setting the glass down she caught something flashing from the corner of her eye in the living room. Moving to get a better look Colleen felt her stomach drop as she saw the silhouette of a man sitting in the chair, she had occupied most of the day. The bracelet layed out across the coffee table in front of him.

"The breadcrumb box? Really?" Brock's voice came out of the shadow. Colleen swallowed hard, trying to clear the lump in her throat.

"How did you get in here?" Her voice cracked. She hadn't heard a peep from anything out in the living room. So much for her alarm system.

"The way I always do. I figured you would put some kind of alarm system up, so I came prepared for it." He shifted in the chair and clicked on the lamp next to him illuminating the room.

"If you came for the bracelet, you found it. So, you can leave now." Colleen waved towards the door.

"I didn't come for the bracelet Colleen; I came to talk to you." He leaned forward propping his arms against his knees.

"And you thought the best way to talk to me is sitting creepily in the dark in my living room?" Colleen crossed her arms across her chest, aware that all she wore was an over-sized shirt with nothing but a pair of panties underneath.

"I planned to wait until morning, I didn't think you would wake up."

Colleen tightened her arms. "Yeah, well I had a nightmare. Not surprising since my life became one yesterday."

Brock flinched a little.

"I didn't plan this; you have to know that."

"You didn't plan on dating me? Only robbing me then. Yeah that's so much better. Thank you for clearing that up." Colleen's voice had a bite to it. She was getting mad now.

Brock ran his hand through his hair, drawing it down his face in frustration.

"I know it sounds bad, but yes. This is what I do, its what I'm good at."

"Thieving?" Colleen scoffed.

"Acquiring and reselling." Brock said, getting an eye roll in response.

"I make sure to never hurt anyone. I'm careful. I observe the store, keeping tabs on which employees are least likely to fight back or try to be a hero. And I make sure to strike when I know they will be the only ones there, no customers, no one to get in the way. But you, I don't know what it was about you but I couldn't get you out of my mind after. I had to check in, make sure you were okay. So, I thought I would pretend to just be a nice random stranger and strike up a conversation, make sure you were holding up okay. But after we talked at the coffee shop I wanted more, I wanted to see you again. After that, I fell for you. I've never felt like this about anyone before. I fell in love with you Colleen."

Colleen sucked in a breath. He had never told her that he loved her before, and here he was doing it now over a piece of stolen jewelry in her living room in the middle of the night.

"And what did you think was going to happen the longer this went on? That we would move in together? Get married? Have a family? All while you kept robbing places?" Colleen could hear the anger in her voice getting stronger.

"I don't know. I think I figured I'd do it for a bit longer until I could fake retirement from the job you thought I had. Maybe convince you to move somewhere smaller, where we could live away from all of this and you'd never know."

"And our whole life would be built on lies and dirty money?"

Brock just stared at her, answering the question with her silence.

"And what am I supposed to do now?" She asked, the anger turning into pure venom in her tone. "Pretend I don't know what you do? What you did to me? I still have night-mares about that night. Did you know that?"

Brock flinched again.

"Do I walk away? Knowing who you are and what you do? Allowing you to keep stealing and terrorizing people? Or do I call the police and turn you in? Be responsible for the man I love being thrown behind bars for the rest of his life!" Colleen was yelling by the end, throwing her arms out.

"You love me?" He whispered as his only response.

"Of course, I love you, you giant fucking asshole! But I can't be a part of this life of yours. I can't." Her voice broke at the end. Colleen could feel the hot sting of the angry tears building, threatening to spill out.

Brock stood and crossed the small living room. He took her in his arms just as the damn broke and the tears that had been MIA finally showed up.

Sobs racked through Colleen shaking her whole body. Brock held her close, rubbing small circles against her back.

"Or, I guess you can kill me and rid yourself of all your problems." Colleen got out between sobs.

"Shh, I'm not killing you Colleen." He pulled away a little bit to look her in the eye.

"Well, that's a relief I guess." She rubbed the back of her hand against her eyes, trying to sop up some of the tears.

"What if I gave it all up?" Brock asked, his face lighting up with hope. "What if I walk away from that life. I can get a real job and we could start over."

Colleen studied his face, seeing the hope in his eyes also wishing they could make this work somehow. Those blue eyes that she loved to get lost in.

"I don't know." She whispered, watching his face fall. "I don't know how I can trust you again." Colleen sniffled, the tears finally drying and she stepped out of Brocks arms. She instantly felt cold without the warmth of his body next to hers.

"I understand." He looked away from her.

"I don't even know how I go back to work after this. How can I look Roger in the eye, knowing his bracelet is sitting on my coffee table right now? These people you steal from, they are hardworking people who don't deserve to be stolen from."

"He doesn't seem too hard pressed." Brock scoffed turning back to her. "He was closed for what? A day? Enough time to file a claim with his insurance who cut him a check without blinking. Showing the world how easily it is to get in and out of one of the most well-known diamond districts in this world without detection? These businesses have gotten lazy. Imagine if I had wanted to hurt someone? How many people would be dead now because these owners were too busy with their bottom line to keep on security measures and protect the people, they are responsible for?" Now Brock's voice was angry, his hands clenched in fists beside him.

He looked back at her and relaxed slightly at the shock on her face from his outburst.

"I'm sorry." He sighed rubbing the back of his head, his shirt stretching across his bicep.

"I think its best if you leave." Colleen said, feeling exhausted from the emotional roller coaster of a conversation and the late hour it was happening in.

"Yeah, okay." Brock agreed and moved across the apartment towards the door.

Colleen noticed the devices from her door sitting beside it as if she hadn't put them up in the first place.

"What about the bracelet?" She asked gesturing towards it still sitting out on the coffee table.

"I'll leave that to you." He said simply. "If you feel like you need to turn me in, then take that as evidence. If not; keep it, wear it, give it back to Campbell's. It's yours now. You stole it fair and square." He shot her a crooked smile as he opened the door and left.

Colleen stood there, turning from the door and staring at the glittering bracelet unsure of what to do next.

Chapter Twenty-Six

Colleen had struggled getting back to sleep that night. She had spent hours staring at the stolen item on her coffee table. She had left it there and went back to try and sleep in her room. Except as soon as she tried closing her eyes, she could hear a scratching sound and discovered Mochi trying to knock it off the table to play with.

That's all she needed was the cat losing it in the apartment. Colleen had a hard enough time finding where the toys she purchased almost weekly kept running off to, she didn't need this going into the abyss with them.

After not knowing what to do with it she ended up putting it back into its velvet box and stuffing it back into the empty breadcrumbs box in her cupboard.

Colleen then spent the rest of the night tossing and turning before settling for looking out her bedroom window and watch the city slowly wake up.

As soon as the sun started streaming in as predicated Mochi was back to her demanding self, chirping at Colleen to get up and feed her. Which she obliged, using the time in the kitchen to look if the box was still in its place or if her late night visitor had changed his mind and come back for it.

The bracelet was still there, which didn't give Colleen any relief. In fact, it just twisted her insides more at the choices she faced.

She went back into her room and dressed in an athleisure set she favored. She then got ready for the day and headed out to get coffee. She no longer cared about trying to keep him out when she wasn't home since he had no problem even when she was.

She chose to have her latte in house, wanting some place she could think outside her small apartment.

Colleen grabbed her coffee mug and pastry and turned to find a seat. Her eyes spied an available table but she hesitated as she realized it was the same one she had sat at when Brock first approached her. A meeting she first thought was happenstance and now knew he had been tracking her like prey.

But it was the only table not occupied so she grabbed it, opting to sit in the chair opposite the one she sat in that day.

A TV was playing in the corner, the morning news showing the storm system that was making its way to the city.

Colleen sipped at her drink, enjoying the oversized mug she could cup in both hands. The berry turnover sat waiting on a heated plate. Suddenly the sound of the 'Breaking news' banner sounded silencing the chatter of the coffee shop.

Colleen looked up and saw the main anchors sitting at their desks with somber faces. Carlos grabbed the remote and turned the volume up so everyone could hear it.

"Good morning everyone, we come to you this morning with breaking news. The NYPD has issued a statement that the man responsible for the string of jewelry store robberies has been caught."

Colleen spit her mouthful of coffee back in her cup, choking on the liquid that had funneled into her lungs at the gasp she had involuntarily taken. The anchors continued-

"Yes, the statement issued by chief Ross says that they had received intel from a store that felt they had been being observed.

The task force assigned to this case was able to set up a sting operation spanning several days that was successful this morning when the store was opening. A man they have identified as Reese Chambers was taken into custody and a search warrant has been issued to search his city apartment."

For a moment, when they stated a name different from Brock's Colleen thought they had caught the wrong man. Or at least the wrong thief. But then they had flashed a mug shot across the screen and there he was, blue eyes and all. A cocky smile on his lips. Colleen felt queasy as the coffee churned in her stomach. She was grateful she hadn't eaten her turnover yet.

They had caught him. But how had he let them? Maybe he had been distracted from their fight, or maybe this was his solution. His way of turning himself in so she wouldn't have to choose what to do. And even though she knew it shouldn't, the thought that he had gotten caught for her made her chest swell.

The news went back to the weather and everyone in the shop went back to their own conversations, completely unaware of what was happening at her table.

She quickly asked for a to go container for her drink and food and packaged them up to take them back to her apartment. She wasn't sure yet what she was going to do next, but she knew she needed to get back home.

Colleen wasn't sure who Brock had given a fake name to and if the police would tie him back to her. If they did, it would take them all of two seconds to see her listed in their file as a victim from the robbery and think she was in on it with Brock, Reese, whoever he was.

Her cellphone rang as she walked through her apartment building door, startling her into nearly dropping her coffee. She grabbed it from her pocket and saw it was her mom. Colleen was not in the mood; she was confident her mom had seen the news and wanted to talk to her about it. So, she ignored the ringing and let it naturally go to voicemail.

As she came up the stairs Colleen saw a bright colorful bouquet sitting on her welcome mat by her front door. She stooped and picked it up as she went inside.

She set it on the counter, noticing the card that stuck out the top. She opened it and saw a familiar scroll on the folded-up letter.

Colleen,

I am truly sorry for the mess I have caused. I love you, and want you to be happy so I will do what I can to make that happen. They will never know you were involved, I made sure of that from the beginning. I hope you can forgive me for the lies and the deceit, and for that little thing with the knife. Out of all the diamonds I have ever held, you are the most beautiful. And one day I will be the man you can trust again.

I love you

Brock

Colleen read the letter three more times, fighting the tears back again. So, he had gotten himself caught today as a way of turning himself in for her, just as she thought.

She looked at the flowers, a beautiful spring mix that immediately brightened up her apartment that was starting to get a grey tint to it from the storm clouds that had begun rolling in.

Mochi twisted around her legs, rubbing against her for attention.

"What do I do Mochi?" Colleen asked looking down at the little cat. Her yellow eyes looked up at her, seeming to say "You know."

Just then her phone rang again, it flashed a New York number but it wasn't one that was saved in her phone. Hesitantly Colleen answered.

"Hello?" she asked.

"Hello, Is this Ms. Scott?" A deep male voice asked.

"Speaking, who is this?" She asked back.

"Ah, Ms. Scott, this is officer Getchler, I took your statement at Campbells."

"Oh yes, officer. How can I help you?" Colleen tried to keep her tone pleasant and even as her heart beat in her throat.

"I don't know if you've seen the news today, but we think we caught the guy who held up your store. We were hoping you could come down and go over your statement again. We want to make sure we have all the facts straight. We would have done a line up, but somehow the news got a hold of the guy's name and has been blasting his photo all over." The man said clearly frustrated.

Colleen smiled a little, she didn't wonder how the news caught wind.

"Oh sure, I don't mind. I can come down now if you'd like." Colleen offered.

"That would be most helpful. I'll be here."

The officer hung up with her, Colleen again couldn't fight the smile over his plight. Brock might have essentially turned himself in, but it was clear he was not going to make it an easy conviction.

She stared at the flowers, thinking of Brock and their time together. A plan started to formulate; she knew what she wanted to do.

Colleen set the flowers onto a high shelf in her living room so that Mochi wouldn't mess with them and went to get into an outfit more suitable for meeting the police.

Chapter Twenty-Seven

The rain started slowly falling as soon as Colleen left her place. She made the decision to hail a cab. Even though she had put a raincoat on, she knew she would still be soaked by the time she made it to the station a few blocks away.

The cab ride was short and like promised Officer Getchler was waiting at his desk for her to arrive.

They went back over her statement, which was easy for Colleen as she hadn't forgotten a single moment. Getchler seemed disappointed when she confirmed she had never seen his face, so even if she hadn't seen the news, she wouldn't have been able to pick him out of a line up.

As he finished up writing his report, Colleen decided to take her chance. She unbuttoned the unassuming rain jacket she had kept on, revealing the dress she wore whenever she had an appointment for some wall street guy who was coming in to buy himself something to congratulate himself or a colleague on a big contract or sale.

It was a tight-fitting red dress with enough of a V-neck to show off her cleavage in a tasteful way. Today it was a little less tasteful as she had worn her pushup bra that she had to dig out from the back of her dresser from her younger clubbing days. It had been a tight fit, which worked out to her advantage.

She got the response she was looking for when officer Gletcher lifted his gaze from his report. He did a small double take, and she used this distraction to ask her question.

"Do you think I can maybe speak to him officer?" She looked at him, watching him struggle to keep direct eye contact with her.

"I just want to ask him why he did it." Colleen lifted her hand and tugged at her necklace, as if she were anxious.

Officer Gletcher was silently fighting for his life in his chair, his gaze dropped and flicked back up to her face quickly.

"I... um..." He stuttered.

"Please? You can make that happen right?" She stared at him innocently, like she had no idea half her chest was hanging out her dress. She shifted slightly in her chair, just enough for a scrap of lace to poke out along the neckline of the dress.

"Uh, yeah. I can do that for you." The officer stood quickly and hurried from his desk. Colleen smiled at his retreating figure.

In a few minutes he returned and escorted Colleen to a large room separated with a wall of plexiglass. A few other people sat in chairs on her side of the room, each of them talking through the pin sized holes drilled in the glass to men dressed in orange jumpsuits. Small partitions broke up the long plexiglass into small cubbies, giving the parties slight privacy from those they were seated next to. Based on the attire of the people on the same side as Colleen, they appeared to be the men's lawyers.

Office Gletcher brought her to one of the empty chairs.

"The interview rooms are all full right now so this will have to do, plus he already confessed to all the robberies. So, there is no need to have his confession to you to be on the record. He will be right out. Come get me if you need anything or if he says anything important."

Colleen nodded at him "Of course."

A door opened on the other side of the glass and Brock was escorted out by two guards. He had cuffs keeping his hands in front of him, and was also wearing one of the orange jumpsuits, however on him it seemed far less baggy and ugly.

Brocks eyes lit with surprise at the site of Colleen. He was sat in the chair opposite her and warned to behave before the guards backed away and left them alone.

"So, was that dress for me? Or was it to celebrate my capture?" Brock asked not fighting his gaze the way the officer had.

Colleen smiled. "How else did you expect me to get them to let me back here?"

Brock smiled wickedly, still taking in her outfit.

"I got your flowers." She whispered, successfully pulling his attention back up. "They were beautiful, thank you."

"You're welcome, did you get my letter?" He asked, his face losing the wicked smile.

"I did, its why I'm here." Colleen paused for a moment. Reading that letter had made her realize she wouldn't ever stop loving this man. He was hers and she was his.

"I know you did it for me, so I wouldn't have to choose. I knew I needed to come and find a way to talk to you, so…" she gestured down at her outfit.

"I'm not the only one who can come up with plans." He said with an almost proud look on his face, his blue eyes lit up. "So, what did you want to come say to me?"

"I wanted to tell you, even after it all. After the lying, and the hiding I still love you. I will still love you, and I'll wait for you." Colleen gently raised her left hand, and placed it low on the glass out of view from the guards.

Brock looked at her in shock for a moment when the other thing she had added to her outfit before she left flashed gently inside the sleeve of her raincoat. The bracelet only viewable from where he sat looking down her sleeve from her raised hand.

"I love you too my diamond." He said moments before a buzzing sounded in the room, letting them know their time was up. Colleen dropped her hand before anyone could see. Brock stood slowly and whispered quickly before his guards came to escort them back to their cells.

"They may have found Reese's home, but they didn't find Brock's." Colleen now was the one who was shocked as she looked at the man standing cuffed in front of her.

"Come on baby, I'm the master of plans." He gave her a wink adding "I'll see you soon." Before the guards got to him and lead him slowly out of the room and back to his cell.

Chapter Twenty-Eight

She wasn't sure why she was so shocked. Of course, he had houses stashed everywhere and identities no one could trace back to him. She wouldn't have been surprised if this wasn't even his first time in jail for it all. What surprised her was the "See you soon," part.

How did he think he was going to manage that? Colleen wondered if he had already had another piece of the plan factored to prove his innocence, similar to how he made sure no one could do a line up on him.

Officer Gletcher had been waiting for her as she left the meeting room. She didn't miss the disappointment that flashed on his face when he had seen she rebuttoned her coat before coming out.

"Did you get the answer you were looking for?" He asked while leading her back to the front of the station.

"No." Colleen answered trying to make her voice sound sad. "He didn't even remember me. At least he said he didn't." She walked with the officer her heals clacking on the tile floor.

"Don't beat yourself up to hard about it, these men are the scum of the earth. Too low to bother a lady such as yourself."

She gave him a small smile before telling him good luck on the trial and left the station.

The rain was really coming down in sheets when Colleen walked out, luckily a line of cabs was idling nearby and she jumped in one right away.

The storm was so big the city looked like it was near dusk and not just past lunchtime with how dark the sky was. All the cars on the road had headlights that's lights were smearing across the windows of the cab from how much water was coming down.

Colleen sprinted from the cab when it pulled up to the curb and made it inside her building without getting completely drenched. However, she did have to lean against one of the brick walls to dump water from her ankle boots one at a time before heading up the stairs.

Mochi was curled up on one of her pedestals when Colleen walked up, only bothering quick glance up at her owner before snuggling back down in her little ball.

She went into the bedroom and redressed into her athleisure outfit from the morning, the pushup bra getting shoved back into its home in the back of the drawer. But not before she made a small cut in the bottom of the fabric near the wire and slid the bracelet between the extra layers of padding.

"Let's see him find it there." She murmured to herself like it was some hide and seek game they were playing.

Giving the bracelet back to Roger would have just created more problems she didn't feel like dealing with. And Brock had been right, Roger had been reimbursed for its value by insurance and had already ordered something similar as its replacement.

Colleen had even made a special display for it at the front of the store.

But what Colleen wasn't sure is how she moved forward from here. How did she go to work tomorrow and pretend the man she loved wasn't facing a life sentence.

Thankfully she hadn't brought him around to meet her coworkers, all though looking back he probably had something to do with that as well. And she didn't really have any girlfriends she had sent his picture too either.

So other than her parents, no one even really knew she was seeing someone.

She sighed as she left her room and grabbed her phone to order some food. She hadn't really eaten breakfast or lunch, so an early dinner it was.

Colleen finished up placing the order for her favorite Thai food and settled onto the couch to watch a movie and spend the rest of her final day of vacation being lazy.

And she did just that. When the food was delivered, she laid it all out on her coffee table and grazed on it the rest of the afternoon. She had found a movie marathon of a series she had seen a dozen times. She would watch her favorite parts and doze off during the boring bits.

Just as the clock was showing a reasonable hour to go to bed Colleen began gathering up the food containers to put the leftovers in the fridge and discard the empties. She paused though with her foot just stepping on the pedal to open the trash can lid when she heard the sound for the now overly familiar sound of the 'Breaking news' announcement.

Dumping what was in her hand she rushed back to the living room.

"Breaking news this evening, Reese Chambers the man arrested just this morning as the suspect in the string of jewelry store robberies plaguing the city has escaped custody. No details have been released yet on how he managed to escape, but the NYPD is asking everyone to be on the lookout and any sightings can be called in to the number we have on the screen now. He is considered armed and dangerous. We will bring more details as we have them. Good night."

Colleen couldn't believe it; he had actually escaped? And quickly too.

She was standing there watching the news break away back to the movie that had been playing before the announcement. She was unsure of what to do next.

But then a familiar knock sounded at her door and Colleen smiled as she walked over and opened it.

Brock stood leaning against the door jamb in a denim jacket and jeans ensemble like a greaser from an old film.

He grinned at her.

"Told you I'd see you soon, diamond."

The End